**Stephanie ha
on**

Tony had intentionally not returned her calls. His conscience was getting the best of him. He knew he was simply avoiding the inevitable—telling her yet another lie. He couldn't face her with his latest fabricated story?

He pulled his cell phone from the clip on his belt and hit Speed Dial. Stephanie answered on the second ring.

"There you are," she said with her voice full of cheer. "I left you a couple of messages earlier. You must have been really busy."

"Yeah, I was. I'm sorry."

"Are we going out or do you want me to fix us something?"

"That's the reason for my call. I know this is late notice, but I was hoping we could make it tomorrow night."

"Oh. Okay. Sure." She waited a beat. "Listen, it's no big deal. We can get together tomorrow," she said.

"I'll make it up to you, I swear," he told her.

Books by Donna Hill

Kimani Romance

Love Becomes Her
Saving All My Lovin'
If I Were Your Woman

DONNA HILL

had her first novel published in 1990. Since that time she has written more than fifty titles. A national bestselling author, Donna has won numerous awards for her work. Donna was inspired to write novels from her love of reading, which was instilled in her by her aunt Marjorie before Donna even started school. Her early readings consisted of the classics *Wuthering Heights, Jane Eyre, Rebecca* and a host of Greek mythology. She began writing in grade school, penning love letters for her girlfriends to give to their boyfriends. Donna writes full-time, runs her publicity business, Donna Hill Promotions, and lives in Brooklyn, New York, with her family. She loves hearing from readers and can be reached by writing to writerdoh@aol.com or by visiting her Web site, www.donnahill.com.

If I
Were Your
Woman

DONNA HILL

To my agent Pattie Steele Perkins who always
has my back and to my editor Mavis Allen
who welcomed me with open arms.

 KIMANI PRESS™

ISBN-13: 978-0-373-86004-3
ISBN-10:   0-373-86004-8

IF I WERE YOUR WOMAN

www.kimanipress.com

Printed in U.S.A.

Dear Reader,

Thank you for continuing to take this journey with me and my wonderful cast of fortysomething divas!

I hope that you not only enjoyed *If I Were Your Woman,* but were inspired by Stephanie's story. We all have baggage, we all have parts of ourselves and our lives that we'd prefer to keep from view. But often, hiding our imperfections prevents us from growing and becoming all that we can be. When Stephanie and Tony were finally able to open up and free themselves from the ties and secrets of the past, they were able to love unconditionally and completely. As always, Stephanie had her girlz to help her along the way, even as they continued to tread their own waters of love and romance.

Be sure to stay tuned for *After Dark* (Kimani Romance, July 2007), which will feature Elizabeth Lewis and her handsome beau, Ron. There will be plenty in store for them and as always the girlz will be right at her side! Because, of course, one never knows just who may come through the doors of Pause.

Peace and blessings,

Donna

Chapter 1

Stephanie Moore was nudged awake by the tantalizing aroma of hash browns, sizzling bacon, whipped eggs...and were those buttermilk biscuits she smelled? She squeezed her eyes tight and stretched, practically purring in the process. The night she'd spent with Tony drifted to her consciousness, and a wicked smile crept across her mouth.

"My mama always told me if a man could cook and satisfy a woman in bed he could keep a smile on her face forever."

Stephanie's eyes slid open. Tony stood in the arch of her bedroom door bare-chested, gorgeous and carrying a tray fit for a queen.

"Good morning," she said, her voice still slick with sleep.

Tony strolled barefoot across the hardwood floor. The thin cotton pajama pants hanging low on his hips sent Stephanie's pulse racing.

Humph, humph, humph. Nothing like a good-looking man who knew his way around a kitchen. Slowly she sat up. The soft peach-colored sheet dropped to her waist. Tony's eyes darkened with appreciation.

"I don't think your mama would imagine her baby boy doing some of the things you did to me last night to make me happy."

He sat down on the side of the bed and set the tray on her lap, before leaning forward and capturing an exposed nipple in his mouth for a hot second. Stephanie drew in a sharp breath. Tony pulled back and looked into her eyes. "Then it'll be our little secret."

She grinned and scooped a forkful of hash browns into her mouth. Her eyes drifted closed in delight. "Hmm. Wonderful."

"Great." He jumped up and started for the bathroom.

"Aren't you going to eat?"

Tony stopped midway and tossed over his shoulder, "I, uh, have an early meeting. Thought I told you about it. New client."

Stephanie frowned for a moment trying to recall the elusive conversation, but nothing came to mind. She shrugged it off. "Must have forgotten."

He stepped into the adjoining master bath and turned on the shower full blast, then came back and stepped out of his pajama bottoms.

The food stuck in Stephanie's throat for a moment. Damn, he was a handful—gorgeous from top to middle to bottom. He worked out regularly and it showed in the sculpted chest and arms, the six-pack that made her mouth water all covered in a smooth milk chocolate package. When they'd first met over a business lunch— while she was interviewing photographers to do the spa's brochure—he'd worn his hair cut short. But over the past few months he'd let it grow out and wore it lightly twisted on the tips giving him a true avante-garde West Village look, typical of the artsy set.

"If you don't step out of my range of vision you won't be going anywhere anytime soon."

Tony grinned. "Yes, ma'am." He turned, gave her a quick eyeful, and returned to the bathroom.

Stephanie shook her head in amusement. She was happy, she realized, as she sipped her juice, savoring its taste and Tony's thoughtfulness.

Tony was the first real relationship she'd had in years—a healthy one at least. The time she'd spent and wasted with her ex-lover and boss, Conrad Hendricks, was a disaster waiting to happen and it did in Armageddon proportions. A shiver of disgust crept along her spine. It was a part of her life she'd rather forget, but there were still loose ends that needed to be severed—if she could bring herself to do what was necessary.

She put her cup of juice down and picked up a piece of toast, chewing thoughtfully. Even being enveloped in Tony's caring and bathed in happiness, she still found it hard to let go of the binds that tied her heart. Tony had talked about love. Yes, the dreaded *L* word. At the time she'd said something innocuous like "who wouldn't love you?" But she'd never really answered him. He hadn't brought it up again. And she wouldn't dare.

Love. It didn't figure into her life. Not really. She'd been in deep *like*. She'd even been in lust, but never *in love*. Truth was, she wasn't sure if she knew how, or better still, if she was worthy of being loved.

She sighed heavily, lifted the tray from her lap and set it on the bedside table. Her experiences with men had been suspect at best. She'd always been too trusting, too giving, too naive time after time. There was never anything for her at the end of the rainbow except hurt and disappointment.

That's why she wanted to take her time with Tony, and he was either along for the ride or not. She wasn't a kid anymore. She was forty-five years old. The days of doing things without thinking them through were over. She'd paid a high price for her actions and had no intention of overdrawing on her account again.

"I'll call you later this afternoon."

Stephanie looked up and for an instant her misgivings disappeared. But only for an instant. "Okay. Call me on my cell. I'll be at Pause most of the day. Terri is coming by around one." She watched him buttoning his white shirt. Tony loved some white shirts and they looked so good against his skin.

"So you're really gonna take on a partner?" He gave her a quick look while he fastened his belt.

She reached for her juice and took a long swallow before speaking. "Since the opening of Pause, I've been getting calls left and right to do PR campaigns. The spa has gotten really good press and it opened the doors for me. So if I'm going to run a business on my own I'm going to need help to do it right. No way will I be able to handle everything on my own. Terri has what it takes and I think we will make a great team."

"You know I'm behind you one hundred percent. I want to see you fly, baby." He crossed the room, leaned down, and looked into her eyes. His voice lowered to a gentle rumble. "Besides, I get totally turned on by women in charge." He winked.

Stephanie laughed and whacked his brick-hard biceps. "You are too silly."

"That's what all the girls say." His kiss was sweet and tender. Stephanie's stomach did a little dance.

"Later," she hummed against his mouth before he backed away.

He snatched up his heavy camera bag, draped the strap over his shoulder, and strode out.

Stephanie touched her lips with the tip of her fingers and closed her eyes. Yes, it would be easy to let herself love Anthony Dixon—when she was ready. When would that be? It was a question that would remain unanswered, at least for now.

She hadn't realized that she'd dozed off until the ringing phone stirred her awake. She blinked several times in confusion before sitting up and reaching blindly for the phone on the nightstand.

"Hello?"

"Stephanie Moore?"

Must be a telemarketer, she thought through the cobwebs of sleep. "I don't want any—"

"This is Marilyn Hendricks, Conrad's wife."

Stephanie was wide awake now. She sat up in bed. "I told you not to call here again. I have a restraining order—"

"I don't give a damn what you have. You ruined my life and you're not going to get away with it."

"We have nothing to talk about, Mrs. Hendricks. I didn't ruin your life, your husband did."

Marilyn laughed in that manic way loonies do in the movies. Stephanie shuddered.

"If you thought for a minute that I was going to let your affair with my husband, the father of my children, slide by without a fight—think again."

"I don't want your husband. I told you and I told him as much. Don't call—"

"If you think this is over, you are sadly mistaken," she said, her voice suddenly dropping to an eerie monotone.

The dial tone suddenly hummed in Stephanie's ear. Stunned, she slowly hung up the phone, staring at it as if the instrument were the true offender.

"Crazy bitch," she muttered, then vigorously rubbed the goose bumps that swiftly rose along her arms like an attack of hives.

She pushed up from the bed and marched across her bedroom floor, uttering a string of expletives all directed at Mrs. Conrad Hendricks.

Stephanie had never met the woman and Conrad never brought her to any company events, which at the time was fine with Stephanie. She was pretty sure she would have been hard-pressed to pull off an innocent act while chatting with the woman whose husband she was sleeping with.

She'd seen pictures of Marilyn. An average-looking white girl: big boobs, blond and blue-eyed, rosy cheeks and a toothy grin. She looked like she could easily play in a commercial for shampoo or something. Not overly pretty but good-looking enough.

Stephanie went into the bath for a long hot shower, determined to wash all thoughts of Marilyn and her husband out of her system.

It was a little past noon when Stephanie arrived at Pause for Men. The 125th Street four-story brownstone was innocuous enough from the outside, but the inside was a masterpiece. The ground floor housed reception and registra-tion along with a cozy health food café, an exercise room, and backyard dining when the weather was nice. On the parlor floor was the weight room and treadmills, complete with personal trainers. The third floor held several lounge rooms with soft music piped in—a great place to relax and chat. The top floor was a full apartment, which Ellie, one of the four coowners, occupied since leaving her philandering husband of twenty-five years. The basement level held the steam and massage rooms, as well as a Jacuzzi and the Pause office.

Every time Stephanie walked into Pause she was overwhelmed by what four friends had accomplished after a few drinks and a dream. Even in the middle of the workweek, the exclusive spa for men only was busy. After less than a year in business they already had a waiting list.

Drew Hawkins, the security guard they'd recently hired, was at the door. His presence immediately brought to mind why they'd had to hire him in the first place—Conrad Hendricks.

Stephanie tugged in a breath. "Hey, Drew. How's it going?" She forced a smile.

"Busy as usual, but quiet."

"Uh, no uninvited guests?" Her gaze darted around the space, then settled back on Drew.

"Nope." His brow crinkled. "You okay? Everything cool?"

"Yeah. Sure." She started to walk off, then

changed her mind. She looked up at him. "Listen, if…" She shook her head. "Never mind."

He touched her upper arm. "Don't worry about anything, Ms. Moore. Nobody is coming past me who's not supposed to."

She pressed her lips into a tight smile. "Thanks." She gave a short bob of her head to punctuate her appreciation, then headed to the front desk. An instant before she arrived, a hand clasped her shoulder and she yelped in fright. She spun around only to come face-to-face with Barbara.

"Relax, girl. What has you all wound up?"

Stephanie pressed her hand to her chest and shook her head at her own foolishness. "Sorry. You startled me, that's all."

Barbara pursed her lips. "You sure that's all it is?"

"Yes. I'm sure." She took a moment and actually looked at Barbara. "You changed your hair!"

Barbara grinned like she'd won something and did a slow pirouette. "You like it?"

"Love it, very becoming. The short look is definitely in and it does wonders for you."

"Why, thank you, my dear."

Barbara Allen was the mastermind behind Pause for Men, but more important, she was the voice of reason for the quartet of friends.

Stephanie put her leather briefcase on top of the registration desk and leaned her hip against it. She folded her arms. "And what does Wil think about this new look?"

Barbara scrunched up her nose. "He hasn't seen it yet." She lowered her voice. "Just had it done this morning. You think he'll like it?"

"Well, if he doesn't you can always *buy* some hair until it grows back."

Barbara tossed her head back and laughed. "You got that right." She slowly sobered. "We really need to have a girls' night. She added with a chuckle, "So much has been going on, between broken engagements, divorces, new men, old men, we need to catch up. We haven't had a night for just us since we all got back from our romantic getaways. And this place keeps us all so busy."

"You know, you're absolutely right. We do need some 'we' time. How about this weekend?"

"Fine with me. I'll check with Ann Marie and Elizabeth."

"Would you mind if I invited Terri to join us?"

"It's okay by me. What's one more plate?"

"Great. As a matter of fact, she's meeting me here today around one. I'll mention it to her."

"Okay, well, let me get busy. I took a half day from the hospital. One of my regular clients can't make it in the evenings. So I told him I'd squeeze him in during the lunch hour. He should be here any minute."

"Barbara, when are you going to quit your job? You're killing yourself running back and forth like this."

Barbara heaved a sigh. "I know, girl, I know. But to tell you the truth, I'm still in shock about the spa. Some days I wake up and can't believe we actually did it and that it's making money. I guess there is that old-school part of me that firmly believes never to put all my eggs in one basket. My job at the hospital is secure. But even though I hit fifty, I'm too young to retire and get my full pension. Anyway, I love what I do. I like my coworkers." She shrugged. "So I guess I'll do both for as long as I can."

"Hmm, that makes sense especially about the retirement part and wanting to ensure your future." She looked into Barbara's all-wise eyes. "That's why it's so important for me to make my own business work. I want that same kind of security, ya know." Her eyes zipped around the room.

"I totally understand, sis. And we're behind you. So don't even worry about it. How is everything working out?"

"Well, once Terri and I work out the terms of our partnership we can get busy." She pulled in a breath and shifted her weight from one foot to the other. "I have several clients pending and of course we still have the 'Pause Man' campaign."

Barbara tilted her head to the right side. "Are you sure something isn't bothering you, Steph? You seem edgy."

"No, really, I'm fine." It was bad enough that the reason why they had to hire security for the spa was that Conrad decided to show up there and they didn't want any trouble. The last thing she needed the girls to know was that she was still being harassed, maybe threatened by his wife now. She told them weeks ago that she was going to have her number changed. But she hadn't gotten around to it. She'd figured that once they were served with the restraining order, her harassing phone calls and Conrad's impromptu visits would stop. She'd stayed at Tony's place for a few weeks and had only recently started staying back at her own apartment.

"Well, for the record, I don't believe you. So if and when you want to talk, I'm ready to listen." She gave her a smile and a pat on the shoulder before walking off toward the massage rooms on the lower level.

Stephanie took a moment to pull herself together, grabbed her briefcase from on top of the registration desk, and walked toward the office to prepare for her meeting with Terri.

When she opened the office door she was surprised to find Ann Marie sitting behind the desk on the phone. Her back was to the door, but she spun the swivel chair around to face Stephanie. She gave her a smile and a thumbs-up signal.

Stephanie angled her head in question, then eased the door closed and took a seat opposite Ann Marie.

Ann Marie flashed a self-satisfied grin on her cherub face when she finished with her call.

"Well, you can t'ank me now or you can t'ank me lata."

"What exactly am I thanking you for?"

"I used all me skills and contacts and found you an office for your business for cheap!" She grinned triumphantly.

"An office?" Her stomach muscles knotted. On any other day it would have been fabulous news.

"Yes, chile, an office. You can't run a real business in this tiny box. How're you going to entertain your big-time clients?"

Ann Marie had been instrumental in getting Stephanie's business license and supporting her dream of starting her own PR company after she'd quit her job at H. L. Reuben. Of all the girls, it was Ann Marie who surprised her most when she'd come to her aid and encouraged her to step out on faith. Over the years she and Ann Marie had been like oil and water.

At times she thought it was simply Ann Marie's feisty Jamaican roots that rubbed her the wrong way. But Ann Marie had changed, she'd mellowed, the bristle around her edges had softened. As a result Stephanie lowered the barrier she'd kept between herself and Ann Marie and they'd finally become real girlfriends.

Stephanie tossed her head. Her shoulder-length weave fell into perfect waves to frame her face. She held up her hand. "Wait, you got me an office?"

"You goin' deaf? That's what me said, mon." She sucked her teeth in mock annoyance.

Stephanie pushed out a breath. "Ann, I don't know if I'm ready...for an office." Her voice faded with each word.

Ann Marie frowned and leaned forward. "I thought you would be excited. Ya look like someone stole something from ya."

Stephanie tried to play it off, but it was too much trouble. She glanced over her shoulder to be sure the door was closed. She drew her chair closer to the table, the wooden legs scraping across the floor.

"I got a call today."

"From who?"

"Conrad's wife."

"Oh, damn." She threw her hands up in the air. "What she wan' now? Guess law and order don't mean not'ing to 'er." She jumped up from her seat and began pacing, her high heels popping like bullets against the floor. She stopped in midstep and swung a look at Stephanie. "Well, what 'appened?"

"I mean she said the same crap she's been saying except…"

"Except what?"

"I don't know, Ann," she said, sounding defeated. "It was different. Kinda scary. I haven't been able to shake it all morning." She visibly shuddered, then looked up at Ann Marie. "To tell you the truth—and not that I don't appreciate your efforts, but I'd just feel safer—here for a while."

Ann Marie pursed her lips and blew out a measured breath then slowly sat back down. "Did she threaten you?"

"Not anything like an 'I'm gonna kill you' kind of threat, but…she said it wasn't over. The thing is it's not so much what she said, but how she said it. It was creepy."

"Did you tell Tony?"

She shook her head. "He'd already left for work. He had a meeting with a new client."

"Listen, she can't be crazy enough to really bother you. You have a restraining order against 'er. Call the police and let them know."

"I want the whole thing to go away!" She slapped her palm down on the table. "Damn it." She covered her face with her hands.

Ann Marie got up and came around to the other side of the table. She knelt down next to Stephanie. "It's going to be okay. The office space can wait." She waved her hand in dismissal. "You can't let 'er get to you."

"I know, I know." She lifted her head toward the ceiling. "I'm just being silly. Probably PMS."

Ann Marie pushed herself up to a standing position. "Yeah, that's probably it." She squeezed her shoulder.

There was a light knock on the door.

"Oh, that's probably Terri," Stephanie said, sniffing hard, then shaking her head. She drew in a breath and stood up. She went to the door and opened it. "Hi, Terri. Right on time."

"Traffic as usual was murder. I was sure I was going to get here for the dinner rush." She stepped in. "Ann Marie, good to see you again."

"I'm always happy to see a woman who can come up with brilliant ideas to bring handsome men right to my doorstep."

The women laughed. The Pause Man

campaign had been such an overwhelming success they'd had to extend the deadline. The concept was that the Pause Man would actually represent the spa. He would have to be not only good to look at, but physically fit, nutrition oriented, and willing to be a spokesman, so he had to have personality as well. Terri had been able to get the backing of major sponsors as part of the prize package.

"I aim to please," Terri said.

"I have an appointment to show a house in an hour. I better get moving," Ann Marie said, slipping into her broker mode. "Take care, Terri." She looked at Stephanie. "Don't forget what I said."

"I won't."

Ann Marie walked out.

Terri turned to Stephanie. "Everything okay? I feel like I walked in on something."

"No, everything is fine. Just going over some spa stuff."

Terri took off her coat and sat down. "So...let's get the campaign stuff out of the way and talk business."

Stephanie brightened. "Yes, let's."

* * *

"When are we going to see you again, Tony?" Leslie stood in the frame of her front door.

"I'll try to get back out here next month, sis."

"Next month! Tony…you gotta do better than this. Your daughter needs you. I'm tired of lying to her about where you are, why you can't stay when you do decide to drop by. She's just a little girl, Tony. It's bad enough that she lost her mother. She may as well have lost you, too!"

"I'm doing the best I can," he shot back.

Leslie looked at her brother with a mixture of love and fury.

"Your best isn't good enough," she said, her voice heavy with disappointment. She shut the door before he could respond.

Slowly Tony turned from the door and walked down the three steps to the paved walkway that led to the street. It was a two-to-three-hour drive back to the city from Connecticut. He generally used that time to decompress after spending the few stolen hours with his daughter, Joy. But it was getting harder, harder now that he was involved with Stephanie.

Before he met her it had been easy to move

through his days, never having to explain the times he disappeared. Now he'd found himself lying. He didn't like it. But what choice did he have? With Stephanie being the kind of woman she was and the sacrifices she'd made for her sister, Samantha, she would never understand. Never understand how a father could abandon his daughter because he couldn't look at her without seeing that her very existence was the result of her mother's death and it was all his fault.

Chapter 2

"So bring me up to speed on the campaign," Stephanie began.

Terri opened a folder on top of the desk. "To date we have 460 entries. They cover the strata, which is great. I'll spend the next two weeks doing the eliminations. I want to have the two finalists and a winner by Valentine's Day. I think that would be a perfect time to make the media announcement."

Stephanie nodded in agreement. "Sounds great. I know you could use some help, but we don't want there to be any shouts of unfair if staff from the spa are involved in the judging."

"Exactly. It's not a problem. I can handle it. And what red-blooded woman wouldn't want to look at pictures of good-looking men all day?"

"I hear that. So the campaign is under control. Next on the agenda is *our* business. As I mentioned in the beginning, when I did the campaign for the spa's opening, we got mega media coverage and it brought a whole host of potential business knocking at my door. It would be great to reap all the benefits myself, though I know that would not only be stupid on my part but it would be business suicide." She paused. "We both have strong PR backgrounds, but you have more strength in marketing. I, on the other hand, can make you believe the earth is really spinning in the opposite direction."

Terri cracked up laughing. "That's the move, girl."

"So I figure that between the two of us, we can't help but win. I have my business license. The business is in my name and if you're willing to come on board, I'd be willing to make you a partner after a year of working together." She'd thought about making a Terri a partner from the beginning, but she didn't want to risk the chance that things wouldn't work out and then get ugly between them.

Terri puckered her lips in thought. "I've already left my job since I'm seeing Michael on a regular basis now. I have plenty of money saved. So that's not an issue." She focused on Stephanie. "How about this? How about we work on projects together as long" —she raised a finger to make a point— "as I can still freelance? I get a commission from you for the things we do together, based on the value of the job, and at the end of the year we take a look at the partner thing and see how we feel." She leaned back in her chair and waited.

She couldn't think of a better offer if she'd come up with it herself. It was perfect, support without lifelong commitment. The best part was that with Terri still doing her own thing, there was no real need for an office—at least not now.

"Sounds more than fair to me. I can have a letter of agreement drafted for you to take a look at…say next week."

"Not a problem."

Stephanie leaned forward, bracing her forearms on the desk. "Not to get all up in your business, but how are things going with you and Michael?"

Michael Townsend was a partner at Sterns and Blac, a major player in the media game. According to the little that Terri had divulged, there were major no-nos with regard to relationships between staff members, particularly upper management and employees. Terri felt so strongly about pursuing her relationship with Michael that she'd recently resigned from her job to make it happen—*after* she'd won the annual competition—which was the whole Pause Man campaign.

Terri beamed. "Things are going great. Different but great. After we spent that weekend together during the holidays, it's been full steam ahead. I'm happy, really happy. I do miss going into the office. But now my reward at the end of the day is a helluva lot better than just punching out!"

"I'm glad to hear it. I know how difficult it can be with on the job love affairs." She glanced away.

"You have experience, I take it?"

"Yes, and I have nothing good to report," she said, trying to make light of it. "But I'm glad things are working out for you."

"If you ever want to talk about it…"

Stephanie forced a smile. "I'll keep that in mind. By the way, are you busy this weekend?"

"Hmm, nothing special. Why?"

"The girls are getting together for a long-overdue girls' night over at Barbara's house and we'd love for you to join us."

Terri's eyes widened in surprise. "Really? Wow. Thanks. Can I let you know before the end of the week?"

"Sure. Just give me a call."

Terri nodded and began collecting her papers. "I will." She stood, then reached for her coat. "I'll keep you posted on how the eliminations are coming along." She draped her coat over her arm.

Stephanie came from behind the desk. "I'll walk you out."

When they reached the main floor, Elizabeth was just stepping behind the front desk.

"Hey, Ellie, you remember Terri."

"Of course. How are you? How's the campaign going?"

"Things are going great. I was just telling Stephanie that I hope to have the finalists weeded out by the end of the month so that we can make a Valentine's Day announcement."

"That would be perfect. I'm excited to see who makes the cut. I told Ron he needs to enter, but he wouldn't hear of it." She laughed.

"Ron was our contractor when we were getting the spa together. He decided to fix a little more than hardwood floors and plumbing." Stephanie winked at Elizabeth.

"Girl, you need to stop." She giggled, then looked at Terri and lowered her voice. "But she's right. And he makes sure all the parts are working on a regular basis."

Stephanie shook her head in amusement. "Ellie, you are getting to be too much. Come on, Terri, before she tells us more than we need to know."

Terri waved goodbye. "See you, Elizabeth, and don't hurt that man!"

"I really like your friends," Terri said as they approached the door.

"Yeah, they're pretty special. So hopefully you can join us on Friday and get to know them."

"I'll certainly try."

Drew opened the door for them and helped Terri into her coat. "Have a nice day."

"Thank you. You do the same." She turned to Stephanie. "I'll call you."

Stephanie watched for a moment as Terri got into her BMW and pulled off.

With that bit of business out of the way and nothing imminent to distract her, she was again faced with her own dilemma. She'd have to tell Tony and she knew immediately what his reaction was going to be. *Go to the police.* She heaved a sigh and walked back toward the office. Maybe it was just a onetime event. Marilyn had a moment of stupidity and that would be the end of it.

For now she'd leave it alone. But if that crazy woman contacted her again—it was on.

It was close to five by the time Tony got back into the city. He thought about going straight to the spa, sweeping Stephanie off her feet, and taking her to a romantic dinner. She'd left him

two messages on his cell phone and he'd intentionally not returned her calls. His conscience
was getting the best of him. He knew he was
simply avoiding the inevitable—another lie. But
the phone was certainly easier than looking her
in the face with his latest fabricated story.

He tossed his camera bag onto the couch,
rotated his stiff neck, and went to the kitchen for
a bottle of water. He chugged it down as he went
over in his head what he was going to tell Stephanie. They were supposed to be getting together
tonight, but he knew he wasn't up for it.

He pulled his cell phone from the clip on his
belt and hit speed-dial. Stephanie answered on
the second ring.

"There you are," she said, her voice full of
cheer. "I left you a couple of messages earlier.
You must have been really busy."

"Yeah, I was. I'm sorry."

"So how did your meeting go?" She bent down
and peered into the recesses of her refrigerator.

"Uh, it went fine. I'll know for sure in a few
days."

"I'm sure you knocked 'em dead. Who was
it anyway?"

"Oh, another corporate client. Needs a company brochure done. Wants shots of the interiors, staff, stuff like that."

"Well, I don't see how they wouldn't hire you on the spot. You're the best photographer this side of the Mississippi!" She giggled.

"You're biased."

"Could be." She got an apple from the veggie tray and took a bite. "I'm starved. Are we going out or do you want me to fix us something?"

"That's the other reason for my call. I know this is late notice, but I was hoping maybe we could make it tomorrow night. I'm really beat."

Stephanie frowned. "Oh. Okay. Sure." She waited a beat. "I guess that means you're not coming by tonight either."

"If you really want me to I can, but I wouldn't be much good." He feigned a yawn.

"You sound tired. Listen, it's no big deal. Get some rest and we can get together tomorrow."

"I'll make it up to you, I swear."

"I'm going to hold you to that."

"I know you will. I'll give you a call tomorrow. Are you going to be around?"

"I do have an appointment in the morning. After that I'll be at the spa."

"I'll call you after lunch and we can decide what we want to do then."

"Sounds good."

He yawned again.

"I'm hanging up before you fall asleep on me."

"I'm sorry. We'll talk tomorrow."

"Rest well."

"Thanks." He disconnected the call.

Tony stood there with the phone in his hand. He was going to have to tell her sooner or later about Joy. But when he did, he knew it would mean becoming something that he couldn't—a father. He hadn't accepted his role in five years and he didn't think he would anytime soon.

Stephanie meandered into her bedroom, plopped down on her bed, and aimed the remote at the television. A stream of images flashed in front of her as she aimlessly surfed. She finally settled on a Lifetime episode, *Presumed Innocent.*

It was probably best that Tony hadn't come by,

she thought. She didn't want to have to tell him about Marilyn's phone call because without a doubt Tony would be a man and feel that he must fix it. And fix it would be calling the police.

It was Tony who'd finally convinced her to take out the restraining order in the first place. He'd even driven her to the courthouse.

The more she thought about it, the more she realized what a good guy Tony Dixon was. He was caring, sexy as all hell, talented, funny, could outcook her with his eyes closed, and most of all he was honest. That's what she appreciated the most.

She'd lived a life of deceit for two years with Conrad. She lied to herself, lied to her friends. No more. As a matter of fact, first thing tomorrow she was going to tell Tony what happened.

The scene on the television caught her attention.

It was Bonnie Bedilia facing her on-screen husband, Harrison Ford, as she calmly, dispassionately explained to him why she had no choice but to murder his mistress. She never thought that he would get blamed for it.

Stephanie felt a jolt and aimed the remote, finally landing on Home Shopping Network. She shook her head. She was being silly, totally over-reacting. She glanced at the phone next to the bed, reached for it, and took it off the hook.

When her doorbell suddenly rang a half hour later, her already stiff spine nearly snapped in half. She scrambled from the bed and darted up front to the intercom. Her mind raced through a montage of scenarios—all of which ended with a showdown between her and Marilyn and her winding up on the eleven o'clock news.

Stephanie pressed Talk. "Who?"

"Why you not answering ya damned phone?"

She released a sigh of relief. She buzzed the lobby door. Moments later Ann Marie was standing at her front door with a bottle tucked under her arm.

"How do you know I'm not busy?" Stephanie challenged as Ann Marie, barely reaching Stephanie's shoulder, brushed by her.

"If you were, you wouldn't have answered your door either." She winked at Stephanie, took off her coat, and muttered something about the growing cold outside, then proceeded to make herself comfortable on the couch. "So…did you tell him?"

Stephanie averted her gaze. "No. I would have…maybe…but he was too tired to come over tonight. I figured it could wait."

"Hmm," Ann Marie murmured. "No more calls?"

"No."

"Good. I know you may not like this, but I spoke to Sterling about it."

Sterling Chambers was the man who finally captured the tough heart of Ann Marie Dennis and forever wrenched her away from the memory of her ex-husband, Terrance Bishop.

Stephanie rolled her eyes and shook her head. "Don't you keep anything secret from that man?"

Ann Marie grinned. "Only where I learned some of my bedroom tricks." She winked.

"You are terrible." She sat down. "Well, since you spilled the beans, what did your live-in attorney say?"

"'Im say a restraining order is only a piece of paper and if someone really wants to get to a person a piece of paper won't stop them."

Stephanie's brows rose and fell. "Gee, that's comforting," she said, full of sarcasm.

"That's why me stop by, won' make sure you're okay."

"Thanks, I appreciate it."

"'Im also say, when a piece of paper fail, boyfriends, big brothers, and fathers can make a difference."

"That lets me out on all counts…except for the boyfriend part. But I don't want Tony going around threatening anyone."

"No brothers?"

"No. Just me and Samantha."

"What about your dad? I never hear you talk about 'im."

Stephanie drew herself up. "Nothing to talk about, really. He's been gone so long that if he ran me over with a truck I wouldn't know who he was."

"Oh, I'm sorry."

"It's okay. It's been a long time. He was never in my life."

"It's hard on boys not having their pops, but it's hard on girls, too." She smiled sadly. "Your pops is a girl's first love. I know not having her pop around affected Raquel. For years I felt guilty about taking her away from Jamaica and her family there. But it was either save myself or turn my soul over to Terrance. I chose to save my soul."

"I always wondered if the decisions I'd made about men and relationships had anything to do with not having a father around."

Ann Marie shrugged. "Could be."

"Well, I'd prefer not to travel down that particular memory lane. What's in the bag?"

Ann Marie took out the bottle of Alize and put it ceremoniously on the center of the smoked-glass coffee table. "I know it's your favorite."

"Let me break out the glasses."

They shared a couple of glasses of wine and chatted about inconsequential things and about getting together on Friday before Ann Marie announced that she needed to be getting home.

Stephanie walked her to the door. "Thanks, Ann."

Ann Marie looked up at Stephanie. "For what?"

"For coming by, bringing wine, being a friend."

Ann Marie waved her hand. "Oh, chile, please, I was in the neighborhood and Sterling only drinks cognac."

Stephanie smiled, knowing the truth behind the words. Ann Marie was really a good person beneath her tough girl exterior.

"Tell him I said hello."

Ann Marie waved and walked out. Stephanie slowly closed the door. With the impromptu visit from Ann, the two glasses of wine, and mindless girl talk, she found herself actually feeling relaxed for the first time since she woke up. Maybe she'd get a good night's sleep after all.

She turned out the lights in the front of the apartment and walked off toward her bedroom.

A light snow had begun to fall. From the car parked out front, he watched the lights go out. He'd seen Ann Marie when she went in, watched her leave, and assumed that Stephanie was now alone. He knew he shouldn't have come here. He had no right, not after everything that had happened. Stephanie had every right to hate him. All he wanted was a chance to make things right between them—when the time was right. He'd learned how to be patient.

Sighing heavily but resigned, he turned on the ignition and headlights, then drove off.

Chapter 3

"Please tell me that was the last guest for the day," Elizabeth said to Carmen, the part-time receptionist. She plopped down on the stool next to Carmen behind the desk.

"Yes, Mrs. Lewis."

"Oh, please," Ellie said with a chuckle, "don't call me Mrs. Lewis. It makes me feel so old."

Carmen grinned, flashing incredible dimples. "I'll keep that in mind. Do you want me to close up?"

"No, I'll finish up. I'm meeting someone in about a half hour."

"Okay. The day's receipts from the café are tallied and in the safe. I must have taken at least a dozen calls about membership. I put the list in the pending file."

Elizabeth blew out a breath. "And the beat goes on, as the Whispers would say."

Carmen frowned in confusion.

Elizabeth waved her hand in dismissal. "Before your time. Go on home, get some rest. Looks like we're going to have a bit of snow before the night is over. Maybe that will keep some of the fellas at home tomorrow."

"Doubt it," Carmen quipped. "This is the next best thing to a quick getaway for most of them. Besides, seeing a string of men hour after hour ain't half-bad for a day's work, ya know."

"That's what all the girls say."

"Well, good night, Mrs.... I mean Ms. Elizabeth."

"Elizabeth or Ellie is fine."

Carmen drew in a breath, picked up her purse and coat. "I'll get it together. Promise." She waved goodbye and headed for the door.

Elizabeth was exhausted. When she'd told the girls that she was willing to manage Pause, she didn't imagine that it would be quite the booming success that it had become and all the work that it would entail. She was the only one of the quartet who actually worked at the spa full-time. Not to mention that she lived on the top floor. At times she felt that she lived and breathed Pause for Men. She was looking forward to getting away even if it was only to have dinner at her twin daughters' restaurant.

She checked her watch. Ron would be there to pick her up in about an hour. She wanted to do a quick check of the premises and hopefully get a chance to freshen up before he arrived.

Elizabeth started in the basement, made sure all the machines were turned off and the used towels were in the bins for pickup by the laundry service in the morning. The café on the first floor was locked up tight, and the exercise rooms were in order. She wiped down the machines with disinfectant, then went upstairs to the lounge. Satisfied, she hurried upstairs to her top-floor apartment, took a quick shower, and changed into a pair of jeans and a sweater.

Looking at herself in the mirror she had to shake her head in amazement. A year ago, she wouldn't have thought twice about putting on a pair of jeans to go out—at least no farther than the corner store. But since her emancipation from her twenty-five-year marriage to Matthew, a lot about her had changed. She owed it all to Ron. He introduced a side of her that she had buried under the guise of what she believed a wife should be: a good homemaker, mother, and dutiful wife. Her entire existence for more than two decades had been dedicated to her family and keeping a pristine home.

At times she missed the house that she had so lovingly created over the years. But her freedom was worth the loss.

She peered a bit closer toward the mirror, noticed some extra gray around the edges of her hair, and made a mental note to make a salon appointment. She applied her lipstick, just as her doorbell rang.

She walked to the front of the two-bedroom apartment and pressed the intercom, thankful once again that she'd listened to Ron and had it installed when they were renovating the building.

It definitely cut down on the wear and tear of running up and down the stairs to answer the door or yelling out the window—a practice that she abhorred.

"Who?"

"Ron."

She buzzed him in and went to get her purse from the bedroom. No matter how many times she heard his voice or looked at his face, she still got that little tingle in the pit of her stomach and her pulse would kick up a notch. Being with Ron Powers was like being a young girl in love again.

Moments later he was knocking on her front door.

"Come in. It's open," she called out as she came from the back of the apartment.

"Hey, baby."

Her breath bunched into a knot in her throat. She suddenly felt shy and uncertain with him looking at her as if she were the appetizer before the main course.

Ron moved with power and ease across the floor. He tilted up her chin and softly kissed her lips. "Hmm, I've been waiting for that all day."

"Have you?" she said in a whisper.

"Yeah, that and more. But we'll work that out when we get back." He kissed her again before moving away. "We better get going so we can get back before it really gets bad out there."

"Okay, let me grab my coat." She took her tan wool coat out of the closet and a chocolate colored scarf. "Ready."

"Oh, I brought a friend of mine along. He's down in the car. I hope you don't mind," he said as he closed the door behind them.

"No, not at all. Is he joining us for dinner?"

"Yeah. I felt kinda bad. He doesn't have any family or anything."

"A friend of yours is a friend of mine."

The streets were coated in a layer of white, the flakes continuing to fall, the streetlights giving them an iridescent glow.

"The first snowfall is so beautiful."

"This will be our first winter together," Ron said. He leaned down and whispered in her ear, "I can't wait to make love to you with the snow falling outside the window." He nibbled her ear and she giggled.

"Behave in front of company," she playfully warned as he opened the car door for her.

He darted around to the other side and hopped in. "Elizabeth, this is Ali Aziz. We go way back. He just moved up here from Atlanta last month and joined my construction crew. Best carpenter in the biz." He chuckled and turned on the car.

Elizabeth twisted around in her seat. A hint of something familiar struck her, but she couldn't put her finger on it. She supposed she was thrown off by the fact that he was older than she'd expected. A good-looking man, in the "I've seen the world" kind of way. Medium brown complexion, soft, almost sad eyes, sharp cheekbones that seemed to almost cut through his skin, full lips, and a broad nose. He was a big man. She could tell that much even though he was sitting down, and when he stretched his hand across the seat to shake hers, her fingers disappeared.

"Nice to meet you," she said.

"You too. Ron hasn't stopped talking about you. I feel like I know you already," he said in a barely discernible southern drawl.

Ron slowly pulled off and headed for Delectables, the health food restaurant owned by Elizabeth's twin daughters, Dawne and Desiree.

By the time they arrived the wind had kicked up a notch, but the snow had stopped. They hurried inside and were enveloped in warmth and mouthwatering aromas.

Desiree came up to greet them. "Hey, Mom." She kissed her cheek, then turned to Ron and gave him a quick hug. "Good to see you," she said to him.

"This is my friend Ali Aziz. He works on the crew. Ali, this is one of the twins." He chuckled. "I'm still working on telling them apart."

Desiree stuck out her hand. "I'm Desiree Lewis. I'm the cute one. You'll see when you meet my sister." She stuck out her tongue at Ron.

"I'll keep that in mind," Ali said.

"I was hoping you would still make it," Dawne said, walking up to the group. "Getting pretty bad out there." She wiped her hands on her apron. "I'm Dawne. I'm sure my sister told you she was the cute one, but that's the lie she tells everyone." She extended her hand to Ali.

He laughed. "Ali Aziz. Nice to meet you."

"Do you work with Ron?" Dawne asked.

"Yes, started about a month ago."

"Don't let him work you to death," Desiree said.

He jerked his head in Ron's direction and smiled. "Tell him that."

"You're gonna give me a bad name, man. Let's get settled before you have them thinking all kinds of awful things about me."

"Sit anywhere. You guys are our last customers for the day. We were getting the menu prepared for tomorrow for the spa," Dawne said.

Desiree went to lock the front door.

"Let me know when you're ready to order," Dawne said, then headed back to the kitchen.

They took a booth and sat down.

"How long have you two known each other?" Elizabeth asked.

Ron and Ali looked at each other as they mentally calculated the years.

"A long time," they said in unison, then laughed.

"I met this guy when he was young," Ron said, hooking his thumb toward Ali.

"We both were. You were no more than a kid at the time."

"How did you meet?"

"At a Black Panther meeting," Ron said.

Elizabeth's eyes widened with interest. "Really? Ron told us all about his 'revolution days.'" She leaned forward, not wanting to miss a word.

"I was heading up a local chapter, and this scrawny kid comes in—"

"See, this is how stories get distorted. I was nevah scrawny!"

They alternated in their storytelling, making light of some intense situations with the marches, the raids by police, and the tension of those days. It was all so fascinating that the meal and two hours had flown by.

"You have to come back again, Mr. Aziz," Desiree was saying as she collected the plates. "It's so rare that this generation actually gets to talk to people who were in the midst of the struggle and what it was really all about."

"Thanks for the invitation. I definitely will. Your place is lovely and the food was really great. Although I'm a steak and potatoes man, I gotta give it to you ladies."

"This is our pride and joy," Dawne said, looking lovingly at her sister. "It was a struggle at first, especially opening up right across the street from a rib joint." The sisters laughed. "But we hung in there and now we have a steady flow of regulars, not to mention the work that we get by providing the food for the spa. We've finally been able to hire some help."

"Nothing like having a dream and finally seeing it come true," Ali said, his voice suddenly melancholy. He shook his head as if to dispel something only he could see and forced a smile.

Ron looked at him for a moment, then stood and helped Elizabeth with her coat.

"I'll drop you off, Ali, after the girls lock up, since I convinced you to leave your car."

"Naw, I'm good. I can make it from here. Why don't you two go on with your evening? I can stay." He turned to the twins. "If you need any last-minute help, I can pitch in."

"Sure. We could always use some help," Dawne said.

"Thanks, Ali. I never feel comfortable with them locking up at night by themselves," Elizabeth said.

"Not a problem. I'm happy to do it."

Ron clapped him on the back. "Okay, take care of our girls and I'll see you in the morning."

"Sure thing. And really nice meeting you, Elizabeth."

"You too."

Elizabeth kissed and hugged her daughters goodbye, then went out to meet the biting wind with Ron's arm wrapped securely around her.

"I can't wait to get you home," Ron murmured. "It took all I had to concentrate on my food and conversation with you sitting right across from me looking like dessert. And, woman, every time you ran your tongue across your lips..." He tossed his head back and groaned deep in his throat.

"Ron, you're crazy!"

"Crazy about you." He pulled up in front of the building and turned to her. "You know that, don't you?"

She swallowed and nodded her head, unsure of her voice.

"Good. Now come on so I can show you just how crazy I am."

"Your friend is really nice," she said as they went inside.

"Yeah, he's a good guy. Got some bad breaks, but he kept it together."

"Bad breaks? What do you mean?" She hung up her coat and took Ron's from him.

"Got locked up on a bad break, spent years in jail, and lost his family as a result."

"Jail? For what?"

"Murder."

Chapter 4

Stephanie was up with the sun, and her first thought was of Tony. It was the first time in weeks that they hadn't spent the night together, and she realized how much she missed waking up next to him in the morning.

She pulled herself out of bed, not sure if this new realization was a good thing or not. A part of her knew that getting that close to someone was not a good thing; you began to rely on them for your happiness, become emotionally attached. And she knew from experience that the only one you could truly rely on was yourself.

Besides, there wasn't enough of her to go around. She had to be there for her sister, Samantha, and that took all the love and commitment she had.

She meandered into the kitchen and put on a pot of coffee, then turned on the radio. Moments into one of her favorite songs by Kem, the DJ cut away to announce a severe snowstorm warning for the entire metropolitan area.

"Damn," she muttered and went to the windows that faced the front. She opened the blinds onto a sea of white. Streets and cars were covered in at least two inches of snow and it was still coming down. She needed to get dressed and make a grocery store run in case she really did get snowed in.

She quickly got dressed, pulling out her heavy cream-colored pullover sweater and a pair of dark brown corduroy pants. It took her a few minutes of hunting around in the bottom of the coat closet to locate her boots. She grabbed a ski cap from the top shelf of the closet and put on her coat.

"Jeez, all this just to go to the store." She got her purse and was checking for her wallet and her cell phone when she remembered that she hadn't put her phone back on the hook from the night before. She made a quick dash back into her bedroom and hung up the phone. No sooner had she set it down than it rang in her hand. She let it ring. Just the thought that it might be Marilyn was something she wasn't in the frame of mind to deal with. *Since when did you become such a coward?* She reached for the phone and snatched it up.

"Hello?"

"Steph, it's me, Tony."

She released a breath of relief. "Hey. Feeling better?"

"Uh, yeah. Listen, I feel really crappy about not getting over there last night. Have you looked outside?"

"I was on my way out the door to run to the store when the phone rang." He didn't need to know that she'd left it off the hook all night.

"Look, I'm going to get dressed and come over. I'll bring some stuff with me. Great day to snuggle."

She smiled. "I like the sound of that."

"I'll be there as soon as I can. Okay?"

"I'll be waiting."

The one great thing about living in New York was that there was a store on practically every corner. A rather well-stocked supermarket was little more than a block away. However, it was slip and go the entire trek. Once she arrived it was clear that her neighbors had the same idea she did. The lines were long and shopping carts were piled high. She got what she needed, but the usual fifteen-minute jaunt took more than an hour.

By the time she inched her way back to her apartment building, the wind had kicked up and the snow swirled in great gusts. She lowered her head against the onslaught and hoped she didn't fall flat on her big behind before she got in her door. She turned toward her building ready to conquer the slippery steps when she felt her feet slide from beneath her. Her brain shot into self-preservation mode. The hell with the bag: *Save butt from hitting the ground.* The bag flew out of her hands as she reached for the railing to the steps. She wasn't going to make it. The bag plopped to the ground just as a strong pair of hands grabbed her beneath her arms.

"We almost lost ya," the deep voice said from behind her.

She gripped the rail, drew in a quick breath, and gingerly turned around. Her knight's face was partly shielded by a hood and a ski hat pulled low over his forehead. The whirling snow negated a better look. He bent down and picked up her bag.

"Thank you," she finally managed to say.

He handed her the bag. " A little wet, but I don't think anything's broken."

"'Preciate it. That could have been ugly." He was staring at her. Her pulse raced. Instinct urged her to run. Her eyes darted left, then right. They were the only people on the street. "Thanks again."

He nodded and started off down the street. Her breathing began to return to normal. She turned and slowly walked up the stairs. Years of living in New York had truly jaded her. Instead of accepting a simple kindness she had him pegged as the next Jack the Ripper.

Once upstairs she got out of her wet clothes and put her groceries away, then put water on to boil for tea and took out the fixings for a pot of homemade chicken soup. It was the one thing she could actually fix without burning.

With her ingredients simmering, and the snow gently falling outside, her apartment took on a warm and cozy feeling. She went into her living room and turned on the CD player, then decided to call Elizabeth and check on things at the spa.

"You would think that folks would have stayed home today," Elizabeth was saying. "But we have about twenty men here already. Unbelievable."

"Ell, I know *you* don't have far to go, but maybe you should close up early. How much staff is there?"

"Carmen is here and Barbara came in. We have one trainer and the clerk in the café. We can get by."

"I still think you all should close early. You won't get stuck but everyone else might."

"True. Ron is outside shoveling now and Drew is helping, but it looks like a waste of time."

"The last thing we need is someone falling."

"You definitely have a point. I'll talk to Barbara. It's not getting better out there."

"It was murder just getting to the store and back."

"Speaking of murder." She lowered her voice. "I met a murderer last night."

"What? Are you losing it?"

"No. I'm serious," she said in a hushed whisper. "I'll tell you all about it on Friday at Barbara's. He's a friend of Ron's. Look, I gotta go."

Stephanie stood there with the phone in her hand, totally unable to process what Elizabeth said. She shook her head. Ellie was obviously overworked. She went to the stove to check on her chicken soup just as the doorbell rang.

She wiped her hands on a towel, fluffed her hair, and went to the door.

"Hey, baby. I would have used my key but…"

Stephanie reached out and grabbed a bag. "What did you do, buy out the whole store?"

Tony stomped his feet before coming inside. "Wanted to make sure we had everything just in case."

Stephanie walked toward the kitchen. "Just in case of what—a nuclear disaster?" She chuckled.

"You just wait. You'll be begging me for those goodies come tonight."

Stephanie put the bag on the counter and took a peek inside. There was everything from snack foods to full-course meals already prepared. "You didn't miss a thing." She started unpacking.

"Told ya." He came up behind her and wrapped his arms around her waist. He leaned down and kissed the back of her neck. "Did you miss me last night?"

She turned to face him and looked up into his eyes. "Just a little." A grin played around her mouth.

"Oh, I see. I may have to stay away longer. So I can be appreciated when I return."

"Think that will help?" She ran the tip of her finger across his lips. He captured it and held it there for a moment. She pulled it out slowly.

"I don't want to find out," he said slowly, then lowered his head and kissed her. He took his time, stroking her cheek with one hand, holding her close with the other.

Stephanie felt light. Her heart thumped against his chest. She moved closer. The strength and security of Tony's nearness pushed her anxieties away. In his presence she felt as if she could deal with anything that life tossed at her.

"You really did miss me," he said, easing back. He looked down into her eyes.

Stephanie glanced away, the instant of vulnerability broken. She shrugged. "A little." She turned her back toward him and busied herself with unpacking the groceries.

"Why is it so hard for you to admit your feelings?"

"I do admit my feelings."

"Maybe when it comes to a client or a new campaign or your friends or the spa, but not when it comes to me, Steph." He stepped closer. "I know that you care. I can see it in your eyes. I feel it in your body when we make love, but you won't let yourself admit it out loud. Maybe not even to yourself."

She felt her body stiffen. Why couldn't he just leave things the way they were? They got along fine, they enjoyed each other's company, they were great in bed together. That should be enough.

"Okay. I give up. I'll leave it alone. I can tell this isn't something you want to discuss." He wandered over to the other side of the room and sat down at the kitchen table. "Something smells good."

"Chicken soup."

"You're kidding."

She spun around to face him, hands on hips, a look of challenge gleaming in her brown eyes. "I beg your pardon."

"Well, let's be honest, Steph, finding your way around a kitchen isn't one of your strong suits." His right brow rose for emphasis.

She tossed a dish towel at him, which he snatched out of the air in midflight. "Very funny. I'm talented in other areas," she said with a petulant grin.

"That you are, sweetheart." He chuckled softly. "Which makes me a bit suspicious about the soup."

"It was the one thing I learned how to fix. When Sam and I were growing up, our mother was rarely around. So I used to toss whatever was in the fridge into a pot and let it boil. I kinda stumbled across fixing chicken soup. But it turned out pretty good. Sam and I had chicken soup at least five days a week. When it ran out, we had sandwiches."

"Sam couldn't cook either, I take it."

"No. Sam always had her head in a book." She stared off into the past. "She could go for hours reading and reading. If I didn't remind her to eat she never would. She wanted to be a doctor, you know." She sighed.

"It wasn't your fault, Steph," he said softly.

She blinked rapidly to clear her eyes that had grown misty. "I've been trying to convince myself of that for years." She went to the stove and checked on her soup.

"At some point you're going to have to listen." He paused a moment. "Is that what drives you so hard?"

"What do you mean?" She put the lid back on the pot, then turned to him.

"Your guilt over your sister. Is that what drives you? Is that what keeps you so busy that you won't give yourself time enough to think of your own life, to feel?"

"My sister needs me. I'm all she has. So I suppose yes, it is what drives me. I have to do whatever I can to make sure she's taken care of."

"Even sacrificing yourself and your own happiness in the process?"

She came to the table and sat down. She stared him straight in the eye. "What if it was you, Tony? What if you were the only person someone you loved dearly could depend on? Would you turn your back for your own personal happiness?"

He swallowed. He could see his daughter's face. See her tears. Hear her laughter. His stomach twisted. "No. Of course not."

"And neither can I," she said, pushing her point home.

He reached across the table and took her hand. "I understand I really do. It's just that I don't want you to shortchange yourself in the process. I want you to be happy." He squeezed her hand. "Most of all I want you to know that I'm here for you. You're not alone anymore."

She lowered her head. "Thanks."

"I'll be able to see how much you appreciate me after I test out your soup." He winked.

"And what are you trying to say?"

"If I make it—"

"Anthony Dixon, don't you say it! You'll eat

this soup and love it. Besides, St. Luke's Hospital is only ten minutes away."

He tossed his head back and laughed. "Very comforting."

They spent the rest of the day relaxing, stretched out on the couch, watching music videos, munching, laughing, telling bad jokes, and talking about the state of the world. In between they shared intermittent kisses and playful touches. At some point during the course of the day, Stephanie had slipped out of her sweater and Tony's pants had come mysteriously loose. The sun had long ago set and the snow continued to fall.

"There's been a project on my mind for a while now," Tony was saying as he stroked her stomach.

Stephanie snuggled closer as an old video of New Edition played. "What's that?" She grabbed a handful of potato chips and pressed her rear closer to Tony.

"I really want to put together a collection of photographs of New Orleans."

She twisted around to look at him over her shoulder. "Really? I think it's a great idea." She finished off her chips. "The whole notion that after more than a year no real progress has been made over there is mind-boggling. And we can't let people forget what happened."

"Exactly. I know I don't have the kind of money or political influence to make a difference at that level, but pictures speak a thousand words." He reached around her to the snacks on the coffee table, dunked a carrot into the dip, and took a bite.

She nodded her head in agreement, trying to stay focused when his finger teased the underside of her breast.

"I thought that once I was able to get enough photos, I could mount a show, use the proceeds to send down to the people. Know what I mean?" He pushed her bra up and cupped her breast in his large palm.

She sucked in a breath. "I think that's brilliant." Her mind raced with possibilities. "I could help you. I could do the publicity and secure a venue when the pictures were ready."

"You would do that?" He squeezed, just a little.

"Of course," she said on a sigh. "It's what I

do." She turned to face him. They were chest to breasts. She smiled and ran her finger across his mouth. "I think it's a wonderful idea." She draped her leg across his hips. "It comes from your heart and that's what'll make it special." She paused, searched his eyes. "It's the thing that makes *you* special."

He reached out and ran his hands through her hair, then pulled her to his waiting lips.

A sudden hunger exploded inside her, taking her by surprise. The driving need to have Tony fill her made her dizzy with want. The hours of playing and innocently teasing each other was like a pot left for hours to boil. She slid her hand up under his sweatshirt, trailing her nails along his chest. He breathed hard against her mouth, then unsnapped her bra from the back. Her breasts sighed in the delight of being set free.

"I want you so bad it aches," he groaned, struggling with the button on her pants.

She pushed his hand away and unfastened her pants pulling them and her panties down in one long motion. Her voice was a harsh, teasing whisper. "How bad? Show me how bad you want me." She stroked the hard rise in his jeans until it felt as if it would burst through the fabric.

All at once she was pinned beneath him. Hot lips seared across her neck, along the rise of her breasts, nibbling and taunting. His mouth captured a hard nipple and suckled until she thought she'd go mad. She writhed beneath him, needing release, pushing her pelvis against him in a sinuous rotating motion.

His mouth moved lower for further exploration, stopping for a moment on her fluttering stomach. A cry caught in her throat when his wet tongue licked the candy between her legs. He pushed his hands beneath her hips to pull her closer, his mouth capturing her completely. He sucked gently on her clitoris that had swollen and was beating like a tiny drum.

Her entire body shuddered. She wanted more, wanted to give him more of what he sought. She draped one leg over the back of the couch, the other she braced on the coffee table.

"It's yours," she moaned. "Take it. All of it."

When his tongue slid inside her, an explosion went off in the center of her being. White light flashed behind her lids as her body shook from the inside out.

"Ooooh, God!"

Without losing a beat Tony thrust up inside her. Her eyes flew open and she stared directly into his. He moved in and out then in slow, maddening circles. "Is this what you want?"

"Yes, yes, yes." She drew her long legs around his back.

"Good. So do I."

He kissed her so softly it could have been a dream. A kiss so sweet and tender, tears sprang in her eyes from the pure joy of it.

They made love in slow motion as if needing to etch every move, every sensation onto their minds forever.

Stephanie felt the slow but steady changes in Tony. The muscles in his back tightened into thick ropes, his thrusts became deeper, harder, more demanding, faster. His heart raced and pounded against hers, his breath hot and quick along the valley of her throat.

She opened herself even wider, raised her hips higher, offered up the fruit of her breasts for him to bury the groans that rose from the bottoms of his feet, the sound a mixture of agony and pure ecstasy.

And then…she was there with him. That telltale heat that pulsed in the pit of her stomach. The tiny shock waves that surged through her limbs. The loss of all reason, her body becoming a conduit for giving and receiving pleasure. The awesomeness of it, the power of it gripped her. Her body surged upward, desperately needing the flames that raged within her to be put out.

Tony expelled a shuddering groan and all the love, the lust, the need to satisfy her rushed from him to her and she gobbled it up with one powerful contraction after another until they were both weak, drained, and utterly sated.

Wrapped in thick terry cloth robes, with music playing in the background and snow falling silently outside, Stephanie and Tony sat in the center of her queen-sized bed sipping on her chicken soup.

"This isn't half-bad," Tony teased.

"Told ya." She grinned in triumph.

He glanced toward the window. "Looks like we might be here for a while."

"Might not be such a bad thing." She winked at him.

"If the rest of the night is anything like the session we just had I'm all for it."

"It was kind of spectacular."

"I wanted you to know how I feel about you, Steph. When it comes to you I can't hold back. I want you to have all of me and I want to leave you so satisfied that you can't think straight." He stared into her eyes until she turned away.

"Mission accomplished," she said softly.

"And there's always more where that came from." He pointed a finger at her for emphasis.

Tony placed his bowl of soup on the nightstand, reached for hers, and put it on the stand as well. He looked at her for a moment. Stephanie felt warm from the heat in his eyes. He leaned slightly forward. His finger traced the outline of the opening in her robe. Her heart quickened. Both hands gently pushed the folds aside. The robe slid off her shoulders to settle around her waist.

"You're incredible," he said, his voice thick

with desire. He touched her exposed skin so softly as if she was delicate china.

Stephanie closed her eyes and drew in a long, slow breath. She lifted the weight of her breasts in each hand while the tips of Tony's fingers grazed across them. He eased her back against the stack of pillows and unfastened the loosely tied belt of her robe. She bent her knees. Tony stretched out between them. He touched her center and found her wet and ready, which only heightened his own need.

He looked into her eyes as he pressed against her opening. "I love you, Steph," he whispered the instant before he entered her.

Stephanie closed her eyes and wrapped her arms around him as tight as she could. She could offer him anything, the pleasure of her body, her laughter, her ideas, her time, her loyalty and respect. But she knew, even as he loved her with all his being, she couldn't give him what he wanted most.

Chapter 5

Barbara did a last check on her apartment before the girls arrived. Her grandmother's dining table was covered with a white linen tablecloth and the chafing dishes were filled with fried chicken, grilled shrimp, macaroni and cheese, fresh green beans, and seasoned rice. There was also a tossed green salad with the plum tomatoes that the girls loved. Ann Marie was sure to bring an island delicacy, Ellie dessert, and of course Steph would bring liquid.

She'd been preparing for hours. She wanted

everything to be perfect, extra special, and not so much because they were welcoming a new member into the tight fold, but because it had been a while since they'd all gotten together, to just relax and enjoy each other's company.

Barbara was just adding lemon to the glass pitcher of iced tea when the doorbell rang. As was tradition, Ann Marie was the first to arrive.

"Hey, girl," Barbara greeted, bending down to kiss Ann Marie's cold cheek.

"Whew, frosty as a frigid woman out there," she quipped, stepping inside.

Barbara chuckled and closed the door. "But at least all that snow is finally gone. Thought we were in Alaska for a minute." She sniffed at the tray in Ann Marie's hand. "Hmm, something smells good."

"Flyin' fish and callaloo. Had to hurry and get it out of the house before Sterling ate it all. Man always meddling in me damned pots."

"And you love it."

Ann Marie's petite face lit up. "Yeah, I do. Didn't ever think I'd want a man around me all the time…but I can't seem to get enough of being with him. Ya know." She looked into Barbara's eyes, looking for understand and validation of her feelings.

Barbara put her hand on Ann Marie's shoulder. "I know exactly how you feel." She took the tray from Ann Marie and walked toward the kitchen while Ann took off her coat and hung it in the hall closet. She followed Barbara inside.

"Wow. What a spread," Ann said, looking at the table. Barbara came in and added scented candles and linen napkins to match the table-cloth. "You can transfer your food into the tray on the end."

Ann Marie followed the instructions of the hostess and added her contribution to the fare.

The bell rang again.

"Could you get that, Ann?" Barbara called out from the kitchen.

Ann went to the door. Stephanie held out her bottle of wine in one hand and a six-pack of Coors in the other. Terri held a covered tray of appetizers.

"Hey, Ann," Stephanie greeted, breezing in. "Sure smells good up in here. I'm starved already."

"I wasn't sure what to bring," Terri offered, following Stephanie inside.

"Whatever it is, we'll be sure to eat it. I can guarantee that," Ann Marie said, closing the door behind them.

"Hello, ladies," Barbara said, stepping out from the kitchen. "Glad you could make it, Terri." She put the punch bowl on the table.

"Thanks for having me."

"Make yourself comfortable. It's all self-serve, so have whatever you want whenever you want it. We definitely don't stand on ceremony around here."

Stephanie took Terri's coat and hung it up with hers in the closet. "Don't tell me I beat Elizabeth here," she called out.

No sooner were the words out of her mouth then the bell rang again. "I got it," Stephanie said.

"Sorry I'm late," Ellie said, a bit breathless. "But I think my sweet potato cheesecake will make up for it." She grinned triumphantly, taunting Stephanie by waving it under her nose as she came inside.

"I vote we break tradition and have dessert first," Stephanie said.

Now that everyone had arrived, Barbara put

the music on low as the ladies sat around playing catch-up and loading their plates.

"I still can't believe that it's been less than a year," Elizabeth said.

"I can still remember that night. We were drunk as skunks," Stephanie said.

"Speak for yourself," Ann Marie piped in.

Stephanie tossed her a look. "If I remember correctly we almost had to pick you up off the floor a couple of times."

Ann Marie rolled her eyes. "Damn Coors done addled your brain."

They all chuckled.

Elizabeth raised her glass in a toast. "To Barbara, who came up with the brilliant idea to open a spa for men."

"Hear, hear!" they chimed.

"And to Ann Marie, who convinced us that hovel of a building could be transformed into a showplace," Barbara said.

"To Stephanie for whipping up a PR campaign that put us on the map!" Ann Marie announced.

"And to our sista Ellie, who holds it down each and every day," Stephanie said. "Wheeling and dealing with those *fine* men!"

"Amen," they chorused.

Stephanie turned to Terri. "And to our new sista friend, Terri Wells."

"Welcome to the family," Barbara said.

Terri looked from one welcoming face to the other. "Thank you for including me. This is all so new to me."

"Whatcha mean?" Ann Marie asked, and took a long swallow of her drink.

"Having girlfriends." She shrugged a little. "I've really never had one—except for Mindy."

"You have four of us now and we can be real pains in the ass when necessary," Ann Marie said.

"You got that right," Stephanie said, and winked at Ann Marie.

"How long have you all been friends?" Terri asked.

They all looked at each other, then started talking at once. Every combination from ten years to shopping mall meetings, to gossiping under hair dryers and everything in between.

Barbara held up her hand. "You know what, ya'll? We never really thought about how we all became friends. Sometimes it seems like we were always friends."

"Sure does," Elizabeth echoed. "I do remember when you and I met," she said to Barbara. She braced her arms on her thighs. "The twins were still in their double strollers." She chuckled at the memory. "I was walking along Lenox Avenue and you stopped me to say how cute they were."

"Yeah, yeah, I remember."

"Then I think you asked me if I knew which way to the library and I told you that's where I was going." She grinned. "While we walked and talked we discovered we lived only blocks from each other. And the rest as they say is history." She turned to the ladies. "Barbara invited me and Matthew over for dinner and we met Marvin."

Barbara's eyes clouded over for an instant as she thought about the loss of her husband. Ellie reached over and touched her hand.

Barbara cleared her throat. "It has been a while, hasn't it? Twenty-odd years ago." She pointed to Stephanie. "We met in Pathmark."

Stephanie tossed her head back and laughed. "We sure did. Place was packed on a Friday night. Ellie was with you, right?"

"Yep. And we all wanted the same cab!" Elizabeth laughed. "Come to find out you lived down the street from me."

Stephanie turned to Ann Marie. "And how did you get all up in the mix?"

Ann Marie cut her a look. "Being the businesswoman that I am, I was canvassing the neighborhood for potential sales. Ellie was sitting outside her house with the twins. They must have been about, what, nine, ten years old, Ellie?"

She nodded. "About that."

"Anyway," Ann Marie continued, "I started talking to her about the benefits of home ownership and she told me she'd been trying to tell her friends the same thing for the longest but they wouldn't listen and maybe I could talk some sense into them. Somehow or other Ellie wrangled an invitation for me to come to Barbara's for one of y'alls get-togethers." She turned to Terri. "And I've been stuck with them ever since!"

They all laughed at the memories, adding little tidbits and anecdotes as they ate and drank.

"Ladies, if Barbara's grandmother's table

could talk—the stories it could tell. We have spilled our guts, tears, gossip, and a few drinks all over it during the years."

"Ain't that the truth," Barbara said, touching the edge of the table with affection.

"Amen to that," Ann Marie said.

Then Stephanie changed the course of the conversation. "Ell, what were you telling me a few days ago about meeting a murderer?"

Everyone's mouths opened, and all eyes were trained on Elizabeth.

"Well, his name is Ali…." She went on to tell them of how they met. "Anyway, he was a former member of the Black Panther Party back in the sixties in Atlanta," she said, her voice lifting with excitement and a hint of intrigue. "During a raid of their headquarters, there was a shoot-out and he was accused of shooting a cop. He was in jail until eight years ago until he was exonerated of all charges. He wasn't even there that night."

"Wow," they chimed.

"It boggles the mind how often our men wind up in jail for crimes they didn't commit," Barbara said. "Really pisses me off."

"And the sad part is, his wife divorced him while he was in jail. Took his two kids and he's never seen them again."

"What a shame," Terri said.

"Anyway, now he's working with Ron on his construction crew. He seems like a really nice guy." She shook her head. "The girls were totally enamored with him and he has such a gentle way about him, I'm sure he would have made a good family man if he'd had the chance. He reminds me of someone, but I just can't put my finger on it."

"Maybe you saw his picture somewhere years ago," Terri offered. "I mean, it was a little before my time, but I do remember there being tons of photos and news clips about the Panthers."

"How old would you say he is?" Stephanie asked.

"Hmm, early sixties."

"You said he had kids?" she asked.

"Yeah, but when I tried to ask about them, he got really quiet. You could tell it still bothered him."

"That's too bad," Ann Marie said. "It would be easy to blame the woman. But sometimes ya gotta do what's best for you and the kids. She had to move on with her life."

Stephanie stood up. "What about the kids? Was it fair to them to grow up without knowing their father?" she blurted out, stunning the group with the vehemence of her outburst. "Excuse me." She walked out and went into the kitchen.

"Touchy subject for Steph," Barbara said by way of explanation to Terri.

"I know all about family loss," Terri said. "My mom, my dad, my brother… It does affect you. And it hits different people different ways."

"I'll go talk to her," Ann Marie offered. "It was me damned big mouth anyway." She pushed up from her seat and went into the kitchen.

Stephanie was sitting at the table, staring into space.

"Steph, you know me run me mouth too much. Didn't mean to upset you."

Stephanie waved her hand and sniffed. "It's okay, really. Any other day it probably would have rolled right off my shoulder." She shook her head and sighed. "But lately, I'm all twisted in a knot. The slightest little thing sets me off."

"It happens…to all of us." She came around

the table and took Stephanie by the arm. "Come on. This night is a fun night, not time to sniff and moan. You can do that later."

Stephanie looked up at Ann Marie and grinned. "Damn, didn't we used to hate each other?" She stood up.

Ann Marie hooked her arm through Stephanie's. "Yeah, we sure did. I still can't stand ya," she added.

They chuckled in friendship and returned to the party.

"Hey, Steph, thanks for inviting me tonight. I really had a good time," Terri said as they stood outside Barbara's building. "You have some really great friends."

"Now they're your friends, too."

Terri smiled. "Yeah, I like the sound of that."

Stephanie gave her a hug. "Get home safely. We'll talk next week."

"Absolutely."

Stephanie started to walk away.

"Steph…"

She stopped and turned. "Yeah?"

Terri approached. "I mean, I know I haven't

known you as long as the others…but if you ever want to…uh, talk about the whole family thing…" She shrugged her right shoulder and let her statement hang in the air.

Stephanie nodded, a pressed smile on her mouth. "Thanks. I'll remember that."

"Good night."

"Night."

Stephanie got behind the wheel of her car, started it, and waited for it to warm up before she pulled off. Then all at once a deep chasm of despair spread through her body like a fever. Tears sprang from her eyes and rolled unchecked down her cheeks. She lowered her head to the steering wheel and sobbed, deep racking sobs, something she hadn't done since the night they pulled her and Samantha out of the car wreck.

She sat up, tugged in several shuddering breaths, then wiped her eyes with her gloved hand. She took a look at her reflection in the rearview mirror, put the car in gear, and pulled off.

Chapter 6

Tony was in his home office in front of his computer putting some digitized effects on a series of pictures he'd taken for a resort. He hadn't seen Stephanie since the two days they'd spent together earlier in the week during the storm. He wanted to give her some space, didn't want her to feel that she was being crowded. But he missed her. More times than he could count he'd picked up the phone to call but changed his mind.

Now here it was, a big Saturday night looming

ahead, and he was home alone with only his computer as company. And no prospect of it getting any better. How sad was that?

He pushed back from his desk, rubbed his tired eyes with his knuckles, then headed for the kitchen. He was pretty sure he'd stuck some pizza in the freezer that he could pop in the microwave.

While he was standing there watching the seconds tick by on the little panel, the phone rang. He went for the phone on the counter hoping that it was Stephanie. A moment of disappointment settled in his stomach at the male voice on the other end, but it was quickly replaced when he recognized who it was.

"Stan!"

"Hey, man. I was hoping this was still your number."

"How the hell are ya?"

"Doing my thing, you know that."

They both laughed at that one. Back in college Stan "the man" Duncan was renowned for his way with women. Rumor had it that Stan had been through the entire senior class and he never disagreed.

Tony pulled up a stool and sat down. "Still in Philly?"

"Actually, I'm on Amtrak. We'll be pulling into Penn Station in about twenty minutes. I'll be in town until next week, but I have meetings. I thought if you weren't busy we could get together tonight—have a few beers and catch up."

"No doubt. Time and place, that's all I need to know."

They quickly talked logistics and set a time to meet at eight in the lobby of Stan's hotel.

By the time Tony got off the phone his weekend wasn't looking so bad after all.

Tony arrived at the Sheraton Hotel on Seventh Avenue and walked into the bustling lobby. He scanned the crowd hoping to spot Stan. Someone tapped him on the shoulder. He turned around.

Stan had that same old grin on his face and his arms opened wide.

"Looking good, looking good," Stan said, clapping Tony on the back. He ruffled his hair. "What's happening with the hair?"

Tony tossed his head back and chuckled. "The new me, man."

"I'll get used to it after a few beers."

"Then let's get this party started."

"Wow, it's been a minute since I've been back in New York," Stan was saying as they were shown to their table.

Barnone was one of Tony's favorite spots. The high-tech design, with splashes of who's who on any given night, always gave him creative inspiration.

"This spot wasn't open the last time I was in town." Stan sat down.

"It's been open about three years."

"Damn, has it been that long since I've been here?"

Tony nodded. "Longer."

The waitress came and took their drink order.

"Hennessey on the rocks," Tony said.

"I'll have water with lemon, no ice."

Tony gave him a questioning look when the waitress left. "Water and lemon? What happened to a night of tying one on for old times' sake?" He smiled at his friend.

"The night is young," he said. He looked around, then focused on Tony. "I gotta do better about staying in touch. But with all the traveling I've been doing it gets hard."

"You never did say what brought you to the Big Hour."

"It's part of a ten-city awareness campaign. I'm actually here with a group."

Tony frowned. "Awareness campaign?" He chuckled. "I didn't know they had campaigns for property managers."

Stan had received his degree in urban economics from Temple University and worked in rehabbing inner-city neighborhoods. He might run around with a lot of women, but he always had a dedication to bettering the community he grew up in.

"It's a little more complicated than that."

"How so?"

Stan shifted a bit in his seat. He had started to reply when the waitress returned with their drinks.

"Are you gentleman ready to order?" She held her pad at the ready.

Stan looked up. "I'll have the house salad to start and the grilled chicken special."

"Steak, medium well, with the baked potato."

"Coming right up." She sashayed away.

Tony turned his attention back to Stan. "You were going to tell me about your tour."

Stan waved off his inquiry. "We can get to me. Tell me what's been happening with you. You still running around snapping pictures?"

Tony chuckled. "Yeah, and finally making a living out of it. I work on my own, starting to get a pretty impressive client list. Mostly company brochures, advertising content, stuff like that. It's pretty cool." He leaned forward. "As a matter of fact that's how I met my lady, Stephanie."

Stan grinned and rubbed his hands together. "Now we're talking. Let's hear it."

Tony leaned back in his seat and began telling his buddy about how he'd met Stephanie when they got together to work on the spa project.

"She's everything I've been looking for, man. Smart, pretty, sexy, intelligent, and she's doing her thing, too. She just started her own PR business."

"I hear a but in there somewhere." Stan looked at his friend over the rim of his glass.

Tony twisted his lips in thought. "I don't know, man…I really care about her. I mean, I love this woman, you feel me?"

"Totally understand. So what's the problem?"

"I don't think she feels the same way. I mean, I know she cares. But anytime I talk about us taking the next step in our relationship or tell her how I feel about her, she starts backing down."

"You think she's seeing someone else?"

"Naw!" He shook his head. "Not Steph." His brow creased.

"How do she and your daughter, Joy, get along."

Tony's face pinched. "She doesn't know about Joy."

"Say what?"

"I haven't told her."

"Why not?"

"I plan to. I do. It's just that it's never been the right time. See, she has a sister…." He told Stan all about Samantha and the feeling of guilt and obligation that Stephanie felt toward her sister. "She is totally devoted to her, man. And I know that if I don't explain things right to Stephanie about Joy and why she's living with my sister…" He slowly shook his head. "She'd never understand."

"You'll never know that unless you tell her."

Tony was quiet for a moment.

"When you were talking about how you feel about her, I heard some hesitation in your voice. Something else going on? If you're hiding stuff from her, what makes you think she's not doing the same thing? You think there may be someone else?"

"No, of course not."

"You sure?"

He blinked and looked at Stan. "What do you mean, am I sure? Yeah, I'm sure." The whole ugly story about Steph and her former boss, Conrad, flashed through his head, but he knew Stephanie would never tread those waters again.

Stan lowered his head for a moment, then looked straight into Tony's face. "Listen, all we know about anyone is what they let us know. Believe me when I tell you." His jaw clenched and he took a swallow of his water. "I've been where you are."

"You? In love?" He laughed. "Not Stan 'the man.' How'd you let that happen?"

"Let's just say I was running and running until I got caught." He swallowed. "Big-time."

He told Tony about Angela. He'd met her at

a bookstore. He was there looking for reference sources and she was attending a signing for some romance author. They both wound up at the checkout counter at the same time and started talking.

"Let's just say we hit it off from the very beginning. A serious vibe, man. We exchanged numbers and she was the one who called first. We started seeing each other on a regular basis. And before I knew it, she was the only woman I was seeing. I started cutting all the rest of them off one by one." He drew in a breath and slowly exhaled. "We were together for a little over a year and I knew without a doubt that this was the woman I wanted to spend the rest of my life with. We were out to dinner one night at this fancy restaurant. I had everything planned. When dessert came I was going to pop the question. The ring was burning a whole in my pocket." His eyes took on a faraway look. "But before I got a chance to ask her anything, she had some news of her own. She was HIV positive."

"Oh…damn," Tony said in a stunned whisper.

"Man, I can't even explain what went through my head. I couldn't think straight. She said she'd caught it from the man she'd been seeing…while she'd been seeing me. It never entered my mind that she would even want to see someone other than me. As far as I was concerned I was putting it down on all levels." He swallowed over the knot in his throat. "But as much as I thought I knew about us and our relationship, I didn't know jack." He braced his chin on his fists, resting his elbows on the table.

"So what about you…are you…okay?"

"I've been positive for three years. But I'm dealing with it. I'm in a good place now, physically and mentally."

"Oh, Stan…I don't know what to say, man. I'm sorry."

"Don't be. I didn't tell you all that for you to feel sorry for me, but to let you know nothing is as it seems. Don't take anything for granted. If you want Stephanie, make sure she knows it. Talk about what both of you want in your relationship, how you want it to go. Don't leave room for guessing. I never told Angie how I felt, what I wanted for us. I figured she could figure it all out for herself. But she didn't. She got insecure and took up with this guy who gave her what she thought she was missing along with a death sentence."

Tony lowered his head and shook it slowly. When he looked back up at his friend he was at a total loss for words. They'd been buddies for years. Stan was invincible. All those years of partying hard and running from one woman to the next with catching no more than a cold, and then when he finally decided to settle down—the ultimate irony.

The waitress brought their meals. Stan snapped open his napkin and draped it on his lap. "So that's my story and I'm sticking with it," he said, chuckling lightly. "But on the real side, that's why I'm here in New York." He looked across the table at Tony. "I'm part of a coalition that makes presentations and gives workshops at schools and corporations on prevention and care. Pretty grassroots, but we're making strides. Which is the other reason why I wanted to talk to you...."

When Tony returned to his apartment he was mentally exhausted. He had a lot to think about. It was still hard to believe that Stan had fallen victim to the great plague of the twentieth century. But it wasn't slowing him down.

He took his time getting undressed as he processed everything he'd been told. But questions continued to nag at him. Why didn't Stephanie want more than just "getting together"? Why was she so indifferent to making a real commitment, to even admitting how she felt about him? Was she seeing someone else? Was that the reason?

Crawling into bed, he stared up at the ceiling. Stan was right. He needed to know where he and Stephanie stood and where they were going, for both their sakes. Look at what happened to Stan for assuming that everything was cool.

Tony flipped onto his side and noticed the message light flashing on his phone. He picked up the handset and punched in his pass code. There were three messages: one from a client, a telemarketer and the last one from Stephanie.

It was almost midnight. He took a chance and called. Stephanie answered on the third ring.

"I just got your message."

Music was playing in the background.

"Oh. Not a problem. I was up."

"Is everything okay?"

She sighed. "Yeah. Just wanted to talk, that's all."

There was something in her voice that he couldn't quite place, almost a tone of melancholy. But he didn't want to read anything into it.

"How about brunch tomorrow? Then maybe we could go see a movie or something," he offered.

"I'd love to. What time?"

"You tell me."

"Twelve-thirty. I could come over there if you want."

"Sure. So I'll see you tomorrow."

"Okay." She hesitated. "Listen, I know it's kind of late but...do you feel like some company?"

He propped himself up on his elbow. "I always feel like seeing you, Steph. You want to come over?"

"Yeah, I do."

"So come on, woman." He chuckled.

"Give me an hour."

"You got it. See you in a few."

He got out of bed, went from one room to the

next and straightened up a bit, checked the fridge, then jumped in the shower.

He'd just thrown on a sweat suit when the doorbell rang.

"Hey, babe."

She stepped up to him, cupped his chin in her palm, and kissed him tenderly on the mouth. "Hi," she whispered.

"I could get used to greetings like that." He put his arm around her shoulder and ushered her inside. "Hungry?"

"No. I'm good." She walked into the living room, set her overnight bag down next to the couch, then turned to face him. "I was hanging out with the girls tonight. We really had a good time. It's been a while since we got together and it wasn't work related." She took off her coat and tossed it on the ottoman, then sat down on the couch. She took off her shoes and tucked her legs beneath her. "What were you up to?"

Tony slung his hands into the pockets of his pants and came to join her on the couch. He draped his arm around her shoulder. "Had dinner with an old friend of mine. I want to tell you about it."

She angled her body on the couch to face him.

"Stan and I went to college in Philly together...."

Stephanie was visibly moved when Tony finished. "I'm so sorry." She squeezed his hand. "From what you said he seems to be taking it well."

"Yeah," he breathed. He shook his head in sadness. "Just so hard to believe when it's someone you know." He paused a moment. "Stan wants me to work with him."

Stephanie frowned in confusion. "Work with him? How, doing what?"

He told her about Stan's tours and speaking engagements. "What he wants to do is to create a visual campaign, one for teens and one for adults. And he wants me to put it together."

"That's wonderful. If anyone can capture emotion and the essence of an issue it's you." She put her hand on his thigh. "You're going to do it, aren't you?"

"That's the part I want to talk to you about. In order for me to do it the way it needs to be done, I'm going to have to start traveling a lot. I'd be gone for long periods of time."

"Oh."

"Are you okay with that?"

Stephanie looked away. She'd be alone. She wouldn't be able to run to him like tonight when she couldn't stand the idea of spending the night alone hoping that the phone didn't ring. But at the same time she'd been ambivalent about a real commitment on her part. She couldn't have it both ways. It wasn't fair to Tony.

"Sure, why wouldn't I be? This is something you need to do. It's important. We'll just make up for lost time when you're in town."

He searched her face, hoping to see something—what, he wasn't sure. "Good. Glad you're cool with it." He pushed up and stood. "Want something to drink? I'm going to get a beer."

"No. I'm good."

He walked into the kitchen. What did he expect her to say? He took a beer from the fridge, opened it, and took a swallow. Did he really think she was going to say she didn't want him to do it? What he did want her to say was that it was going to be hard with him not being around, that she was going to miss him—something. He blew out a breath. But that wasn't Stephanie. She

wasn't the needy, clinging type or overly affec-
tionate—at least not with words.

"Hey, Tony, I'm going to change the CDs,
okay?" she called out.

"Sure. Whatever you want." He joined her in
the room. She'd put on a Luther CD, *Live at
Radio City:* "A House Is Not a Home" was
playing. She turned toward him and held out her
hand. "Dance with me."

He approached, a seductive smile on his
mouth. He took her in his arms and held her
close. The music, the silky smoothness of the
crooner's voice wrapped around them like a
cocoon.

Stephanie pressed her head against the curve
of his neck and inhaled his clean soap and water
scent. Her eyes drifted closed as they moved in
unison with the music.

"I'm glad you came," he said.

"So am I." She tilted her head back and looked
at him. Her heart knocked in her chest.

"I missed you," he said softly.

"How much?"

Tony held her tighter. "Very. Can't you tell?"
He gave her a wicked grin.

"I do believe I get your point." She kissed him lightly on the mouth.

His hands stroked her back in slow up-and-down motions as they danced. She moved even closer, and a soft moan escaped her lips.

He reached down to the hem of her shirt and pulled it up and over her head, only to discover much to his delight that she wore nothing underneath. He tossed the shirt onto the couch. His gaze raked over her. "You are so beautiful."

She unfastened his belt.

"Not here." He took her hand and led her to his bedroom. He pushed the door open.

Stephanie backed into the room, slowly undressing as she did so, dropping her clothes like bread crumbs as she inched toward the bed.

Tony watched in fascination as her perfect form was languidly unveiled for him. He stepped out of his pants and kicked them to the side, then came to her.

Stephanie sat down on the end of the bed and slowly parted her thighs, her eyes never leaving Tony's face. With her right hand she stroked herself, with her left she raised her breast in her palm and offered it to him. He didn't need any more of an invitation. He knelt down in front of her, pushed both of her hands away, and replaced them with his.

Soft sounds of delight hummed in her throat. She reached into his shorts and freed him, the stiffness and weight overflowing in her hand. Tony's pelvis jerked forward in response to her steady up-and-down motion. He groaned, and that only turned her on more.

She scooted back onto the bed and he eagerly followed.

"Tonight is your night," she said before smoothly switching places so that she was on top.

He grinned. "Remember what I told you about women in charge?"

"Oh, I definitely remember." She kissed his lips, long and deep, before moving to his throat, his chest, his stomach. She brushed her lips across the coarse hair, then used her tongue to tease his length, relishing the feel of it pulsing and jumping at her touch.

Tony clutched the sheets in his fists as jolts of sensation shot through him. Then a silky hot wetness enveloped him. He hissed through his teeth as she took him into her mouth and her mind-blowing suckling began. His heart pounded and it took all of his control not to let go.

He reached into the nightstand drawer and pulled out a condom, ripping the pack open with his teeth. Stephanie looked up and grinned. She took it from him and rolled it onto him with her mouth. He was sure he was going to lose his mind then. But the best was yet to come.

Stephanie was in total control, just the way she wanted it. She felt powerful, invincible knowing that she could do this, evoke this much pleasure, make another human being weak with desire.

She positioned herself above him, teasing him some more by hovering over him, only allowing the tip to touch her opening. Each time his pushed upward, needing to gain entry, she pulled back.

Finally, unable to stand denial a moment more, Tony grabbed her hips and jammed her down onto him.

Her head went back and a surreal sound burst from her throat as he held her there, pinned to him, unable to do no more than feel him pulse and jerk inside her. She began to tremble.

Tony loosened his hold and allowed her to move. Now with the freedom she craved, she reached out and gripped the headboard and rode him in wild abandon.

He grabbed her wrists in each hand and loosened her hold on the bed, then eased her back so that her body arched upward and her head nearly touched the mattress. He took a pillow from beneath his head and shoved it under his hips, pushing him even deeper inside her. They both cried out from the incredible pressure that elicited such pleasure.

Shudders began to ricochet through her limbs. The sensations were so intense she could barely breathe. God, this felt good, he felt good. She never wanted it to end—the tingling, teasing, pulsing, throbbing—the thickness, the fullness of him. She didn't want it to stop. She pumped faster, almost in a frenzy, wanting to multiply the incredible feelings she was experiencing. She was on fire, burning from the inside out.

She screamed. Her entire body tensed into one tightrope of raw feeling when Tony pushed the pad of his finger between the breath of air that separated them and pressed down on her swollen clit. Her mind snapped into a million pieces and somewhere in the distance she heard Tony groan so deep and loud that it vibrated through her body.

They lay in a damp tangle of arms and legs, breathing heavily, both caught in an experience that left them searching for words.

Chapter 7

"I was going to fix us some breakfast," Tony said, nuzzling Stephanie's ear.

She wiggled against him. "Hmm, sounds heavenly."

"Good." He snatched the sheet off her and popped her on her bare bottom. "Today, young lady, you are going to learn how to cook."

She pushed her hair away from her face and looked up at him in horror. "You are kidding, aren't you?"

"Do I look like I'm kidding?"

"You look like a naked man who should get back in bed."

He laughed, grabbed her hand, and pulled her from the bed. "Come on, into the shower, then onward to the kitchen."

She got up, stomped her feet like a petulant child, then switched her way to the bathroom. "I'm sure you'll be sorry," she warned over her shoulder.

Stephanie dragged out her shower for as long as she could without having Tony send in troops to rescue her. She emerged from the bathroom in only a towel with the secret hope of distracting her instructor from the task at hand. She knew she was hopeless in the kitchen, and the last thing she wanted was for Tony to see her totally unable to conquer something, even if that something was as simple as cooking.

Tony glanced in her direction when she walked into the room. His gaze lingered for a moment, but he wouldn't be swayed. "As long as you're comfortable," he said in an offhand fashion.

Stephanie puffed out a frustrated breath.

Tony jerked his head. "Don't just stand there looking gorgeous. Come on, let's get started."

She slinked over to the kitchen counter where he'd assembled bowls, knives, seasonings, green and red peppers, an assortment of cheeses, tomatoes, milk…the countertop was covered from end to end.

"What are you making?"

"*I'm* not making anything. I'm instructing, *you're* making. We're going to have a western omelet, whole wheat pancakes, and turkey bacon."

She threw her hands up in the air and looked around. "But…I…"

He took her hands and brought them down to her sides. If she didn't look so terrified he would burst out laughing. "I'll talk you through it. It'll be fun. A team project. We'll start with the condiments."

She muttered something under her breath. Tony chuckled and handed her a green pepper and a knife.

Not only was Tony a stellar photographer, consummate lover, fun, intelligent, and damned good to look at, he was also a wonderful cook and a great teacher.

Stephanie was actually having a good time and she hadn't burned anything. He'd shown her how to make a perfect omelet and pancakes that were light as feathers. They even had a fruit salad. When they sat down at the table she couldn't believe what she'd done.

Tony raised his glass of orange juice in a toast. "Congratulations on a job well done."

Stephanie smiled with well-deserved pride. "Couldn't have done it without you."

"It was my pleasure." He touched his glass to hers.

"Tony." She put her glass down. "There's something I want to talk to you about."

"Sure."

"A few days ago I got a phone call...from Conrad's wife."

Slowly he put down his glass. "A few days ago? What did she say, Steph?"

She repeated the conversation.

His amiable expression hardened. "Why didn't you tell me?"

"I...I don't know. I guess I didn't want you to worry."

He blew out a harsh breath and pushed up from the table. He crossed the room to the sink and turned to face her. "Did you call the police?"

"No."

His nostrils flared. "Why?"

"I just want it all to go away. I knew if the police got involved it would all blow up again."

He looked at her in stunned disbelief. He paced toward her. "This man used you." He bent down in front of her, gripping the edge of table. "He threatened to blackball you in the industry. His wife has verbally harassed you. They have jointly made your life hell. It took months of convincing to get you to take out the restraining order, longer still to make you feel safe again." He spun around in a circle, then whirled toward her. "Forget that you didn't call the police and have them enforce the order." He waved his hand back and forth, then jabbed at his chest. "Why didn't you tell me?" he asked in a harsh whisper.

Stephanie looked away. "I didn't want you upset, Tony. I didn't want you to worry."

He sat down and pulled his chair right up to her. "Steph, that's called being in a relationship. I thought that's what you wanted, what we were working toward."

"We are. I thought I could handle it on my own. I wanted to handle it on my own. But after last night...I wanted to tell you. I didn't want any more secrets between us."

A momentary pang of guilt stabbed him in the gut.

"And...I didn't want to be alone. I didn't want to have to deal with it alone. I didn't want to hear my phone ring and have her on the other end." She sighed heavily. "There, I said it. I needed you." It was more of an accusation than an admission.

He took her hands in his and raised them to his lips. He placed a gentle kiss on her palms. "It's okay to need someone. It doesn't make you weak or less of a person. I want you to need me, Steph, and I want to be there for you when you do."

She blinked back tears. "I've been doing it on my own for so long. I don't know any other way."

"Give it a chance. Give us a chance. A real one."

She stood up and moved away from him.

"You can't let this go. First it will be phone calls. What next? You need to make them know that you're serious. And the only way to do that is to take it to the next level and file the sexual harassment suit against Hendricks. You should have done that in the beginning."

Stephanie folded her arms and tugged on her bottom lip with her teeth. "I'll change my number. I should have done that a long time ago."

"Stephanie, it's not enough and you know it. You've always known it."

She shook her head. "No. This is as far as it goes."

"Do you think it's going to stop?"

"I don't know."

He came up to her. "Look, I know it won't be easy. And it will be hard as hell to handle it on your own." He paused a beat. "Live with me. And I don't mean just on the weekend. I mean day to day, dealing with each other. If you don't want to pursue charges, then put all of it behind you, including the place that the two of you…"

Her head began to pound. Live together? Living together held implications. Was she willing to give up her independence, share bills, daily drama, wake up day after day to the same person? It was happening too fast. She'd never shared that much of herself with anyone. It was easier to keep that emotional distance. That way she didn't get hurt, she wouldn't have to worry about loss.

"It's not something that I want to do." She forced herself to look into his eyes.

"I see. What part, some of what I said or all of it?"

She cleared her throat. "All of it. I'm not going to file the suit and I…can't live with you."

"You want to tell me why?"

"How can I go after Conrad for sexual harassment? I was a part of it. I wasn't some starstruck teenager who didn't know any better. What I did was wrong." Her eyes filled with tears. "He was married. I knew it and it didn't matter."

His expression was incredulous. "Do you hear yourself? He raped you! He should be in jail, for God's sake, and you're blaming yourself?" He crossed over to her. "No one deserves that."

She looked away. "Let it go, Tony."

"If it's a matter of some woman independence thing about you not wanting to move into a man's home, then we can get a place together with both of our names on the lease," he said, ignoring her directive.

How could she explain something she didn't

quite understand herself? She knew she cared deeply for Tony. She enjoyed being with him, but living together…that was asking for more than she was ready to give.

"I can't live with you," she said finally.

He drew himself up. "Can't or won't?"

"Both."

He slowly nodded his head. "So you won't file charges, you won't move out of the place that he raped you in, and you won't move in with me." He chuckled without a hint of humor. "Then maybe it's what you wanted."

She flashed him a look.

"Fine. You've said it all. There's nothing more to discuss." He turned and walked out.

She heard a door slam in the distance and was finally able to release the tight rein she had on herself. She let go a long breath and headed for the bedroom. Tony was sitting on the edge of the bed staring off into space.

"I think I'd better go."

"So do I," he said without looking at her.

She began gathering her things. The silence was physical, weighing down her limbs as she put her belongings into her bag. She got dressed.

Tony still hadn't said a word, hadn't moved from that spot, hadn't looked in her direction.

It was best this way, she thought as she put on her coat. Cut her losses early. She picked up her bag. She started to say something but knew that whatever she said wouldn't matter. She walked out the door without looking back.

Stephanie returned to her apartment and aimlessly puttered around for the rest of the day. She wanted to talk to someone, but there was no one. Barbara had Wil. Ellie had Ron. Ann Marie had Sterling. She had her freedom.

Chapter 8

Barbara felt like a teen on prom night. Wil would be there any minute and she was a nervous wreck. Although she and Wil had been spending all of their free time together and had even gone on a weekend getaway, this would be the first time she had Wil's son, Chauncey, at her home. She wanted to make a good impression on him.

It was still hard to believe that Wil had a teenage son, a son who should have been theirs. How different would their lives have been had she told him about the baby, had she not subsequently lost it? Would they have made it as a couple? And the sad irony was she thought she was helping him by not telling him. He had an athletic scholarship. He was destined for the NFL. But fate had a zinger in store for both of them.

Funny how things turn out, she thought as she fluffed the pillows on the couch. He wound up with someone else and so did she, and after so many years had passed they'd found each other again. You couldn't make up for the past, but you could certainly make plans for the future. They'd been given a second chance to get it right, and she didn't intend to miss a beat.

She was heading for the kitchen to check on the pot roast when the downstairs doorbell rang. Her heart rushed to her throat. She took a deep breath and went to the intercom.

"Yes?"

"It's Wil and Chauncey."

She pressed the buzzer, then dashed to the mirror in the foyer to check her hair and makeup. It would be the first time that Wil had seen her since she'd cut her hair. She hoped he liked it.

She hurried to her front door and pulled it open, just as they'd stepped off the elevator. "Come on in. Chauncey, it's good to see you. I'm glad you came."

"Thanks for inviting me." He walked behind his father into the apartment and looked around. "Nice place."

"Thanks. Let me take your coats."

"I'll do it, Barb." He took his and Chauncey's coats and hung them in the hall closet. "Something sure smells good."

"We're having pot roast. I hope you like it. I should have asked."

"Pot roast is fine. We eat everything," Wil said, laughing.

Chauncey was in the living room.

"Thanks for doing this," Wil said quietly. "And by the way, you look incredible." He kissed her lightly on the lips.

"Thank you," she whispered. "I was hoping you liked it." She nervously patted her head.

"Very much."

They walked into the living room hand in hand. Chauncey was checking out her music collection.

"You like Prince?" he asked with raised brows and wide eyes.

Barbara grinned. "Absolutely. Doesn't everyone?"

"You have some really good stuff here. You even have 45s. Wow."

"Well before your time. The Dells, The Moments, The Delfonics, The Stylistics, Main Ingredient, Smokey Robinson and the Miracles, and of course Marvin Gaye, Martha Reeves, and the Vandellas, The Supremes. They're all there. I even have Mary J, Jill Scott, India Arie, John Legend, Luther. I've always enjoyed music, so I try to keep up. I still can't handle rap, though." She made a face.

"Yeah, my dad can't handle it either."

"Maybe I wouldn't mind so much if most of it wasn't so violent or just plain ridiculous. And the videos..." He shook his head sadly. "Damned shame."

"Don't get him started," Chauncey said, "we'll never eat."

"Speaking of which, are you guys hungry?"

"Always," Chauncey said.

Barbara ushered them into the dining room

while she got the pot roast and put it on a serving platter.

"Need some help?"

She looked over her shoulder to see Wil coming up behind her. "Not the kind of help you want to give," she teased as he kissed her on the back of the neck. His palms curved around her waist as he subtly moved his hips.

"I heard the flame went out on the stove and somebody needed to turn it on." He tugged at her earlobe with the tip of his teeth.

She swatted him on the thigh. "Wil, you need to stop," she said in a rough whisper filled with laughter. "What if Chauncey sees you?" She felt his growing arousal bump up against her behind, and her heart beat a little faster.

"Then he'll know his old man ain't so old and is still getting it."

"Wil Hutchinson, I can't concentrate on what I'm doing with you rubbing up against me like that."

"Oh, really? I'm sorry," he said and rubbed up against her some more. "Hmm, that feels good. Let's forget dinner, get rid of the kid, and run to the back room."

Barbara burst out laughing. "You have lost

your natural mind. Now move out of my way
while I have this knife in my hand."

Wil reluctantly backed up, the bulge visible in
his pants. Barbara's eyes zoomed in. She pointed
at it with the knife. "Better do something about
that," she mouthed before heading off into the
dining room with the platter of food. "And bring
in the casserole dish of rice and the one with the
string beans," she called out from the doorway.
*That ought to keep him busy for a minute and off
my behind,* she thought with amusement. Humph,
she might be fifty but she still had it. Having her
brief but torrid love affair with Michael, a man
young enough to be her son, was proof in the
pudding. She'd almost married him, dazzled by
the attention, his youth, that eye-popping
diamond ring, and his celebrity status on the
NBA. Many a night she'd have to pinch herself
to make sure it was all real. And now Wil was in
her life, confirming the adage that what you may
lack in energy you sure make up for with experience. Wil made love to her as if they had the rest
of their lives to get from point A to point B, and
he intended to use every minute. Slow and steady,
like the mighty Mississippi. Wil's loving didn't

start in the bedroom. He seduced her with a look in the middle of the street, an impromptu massage while they waited for the light to change, talking to her for hours and listening just as long. Wil's loving was as much the act itself as it was getting there. Lord, that man knew how to love up a woman.

"Need some help with that?"

Barbara blinked, then realized she'd been staring into space, thinking all manner of naughty thoughts. Her face heated when she looked at Chauncey and swore he could read her mind. "Oh no. Thanks. Maybe you could help your dad bring the things in from the kitchen."

"Sure."

She exhaled and shook her head. *Hold it together, girl.*

As per her usual dinner guest routine, everything was placed on the mahogany sideboard for folks to take what they wanted.

"Help yourself to as much as you want," she said once Wil and Chauncey joined her. "There's plenty."

They sat at her grandmother's table with their plates piled high.

"Wil, would you say the blessing please?"

They bowed their heads while Wil blessed the food and the cook.

"Amen," they said in unison.

Chauncey dug right in. In between bites he asked, "How did you and my dad meet?"

Barbara smiled at the memory. "We met in high school, through a friend." She stole a look at Wil. "Your dad was much older than me." She emphasized the "much" with a glimmer in her eyes. "Then he went away to college." She hesitated, not sure how much more to say.

"We stayed in touch by phone and letter for a while," Wil said, seeing Barbara's uneasiness. "But with school and distance, we drifted apart." He looked at her and saw gratitude in her eyes for not sharing that very painful time.

"Then you guys have me to thank for getting you back together. If I hadn't dragged Dad to the spa kickin' and screamin' you may never have seen each other again." He took a big forkful of pot roast and chewed triumphantly.

"He's right," Barbara said. "And to think that we've been living right here in the same city all these years and never ran into each other." She shook her head in wonder.

"Well, we're together now," Wil said.

"So, Chauncey, your dad says you work at the Schomberg."

Chauncey talked about his part-time job and his long-term goal of becoming an engineer when he went to college in the fall.

They chatted amicably throughout dinner, with Wil sharing stories of Chauncey's growing up and his take on his latest girlfriend, Missy.

Chauncey looked woefully embarrassed, but took it all in stride. They were just finishing up and Barbara was about to announce dessert when there was a knock on her front door. She frowned.

"Excuse me. Must be one of my neighbors." She couldn't imagine it was anyone else since she didn't hear the intercom buzz. She got up and went to the door. The last person she expected to see stood in front of her.

"Hey, Barb."

"Michael…what are you doing here?" Her stomach did several flips, then leaped to her chest as she looked up into his handsome face. He looked like a model for a men's fashion magazine, his two-button shark-gray suit, the open-collar white shirt, and the familiar heavenly scent that floated around him all lent themselves to his star power. There was no way to ignore a man looking as good as he did.

"I know I should have called. But I'm only in town for a couple of days. I wanted to see you and didn't want to take the chance that you would say no." His light brown eyes rolled slowly over her. "You look incredible."

She tried to swallow over the dry knot in her throat and nearly choked. "Uh, thanks. I'm—"

"May I come in?"

Jeez, her thoughts had come to a grinding halt. She couldn't get past the fact that Wil, her current man, was sitting at her dining room table and Michael, her ex-fiancé, was standing at her door. What was a girl to do?

"Babe, everything okay?"

Oh, damn. She turned to see Wil moving toward her, his gaze zeroed in curiously on Michael. Then recognition kicked in.

"Umm, yes. This is Michael Townsend. Michael, Wil Hutchinson."

Michael stuck out his hand. Wil stood taller

and sucked in his stomach before shaking Michael's hand.

"Michael was in town and stopped by to say hello."

"You missed dinner, but we were getting ready for dessert. Why don't you join us?" Wil asked, with the authority of the man of the house.

"Thanks. I've missed Barbara's cooking," Michael replied, not to be outdone.

Barbara turned toward the dining room and rolled her eyes to the top of her head. *This only happens in the movies,* she thought.

When Michael entered the room, Chauncey's mouth dropped open. He jumped up from his seat. "Michael Townsend, the Miami Heat!"

Michael grinned. He walked over to Chauncey and extended his hand. "You got me on that one. And you are?"

"A fan, I mean Chauncey. Chauncey Hutchinson." He vigorously shook his hand. "Do you know Shaq?"

"Yeah, pretty well." He chuckled.

"Wow," he said in awe. "I watched you the other night against Detroit. Creamed 'em! And that shot you made at the buzzer. Man!"

"We had a good night." He slid his hands into his pockets. You're pretty tall. What, six-three? Do you play?"

"Yeah, on my high school team and some pickup games in the park."

"You got game?"

Chauncey stuck out his chest. "I ain't bad."

Michael clapped him on the back. "Good for you. Maybe I can see you play sometime, give you some tips." He kept his hand on his shoulder.

Chauncey's eyes widened with astonishment. "Get out. The guys will flip. They'll never believe I actually met you." He turned to his father. "Dad, you hear that? Michael said he'd come see me play."

"That's nice, son. But I'm sure *Mr.* Townsend is pretty busy."

Michael looked directly at Wil. "I get to New York quite often." He turned his attention to Chauncey. "Next time you're playing let me know." He pulled a business card out of his jacket pocket and handed it to him. "If I'm in town I'll be sure to stop by."

"Wow." He stared at the card as if it held the secret to eternal life.

"I'll bring out dessert," Barbara announced, snapping the rope of tension that was tightening between Wil and Michael.

"Since I busted in on you guys, let me help you at least." He started after Barbara before Wil had a chance to react.

"So that's who replaced me?" he asked once they were in the kitchen.

"He didn't replace you. Not the way that you're thinking." She kept her back to him as she put the peach cobbler on a platter.

"Were you seeing him while we were together?"

She spun toward him, a resolute expression on her face. "No," she lied through her teeth. One thing a woman never did was confess an indiscretion to another man, even if the relationship was over. That afternoon of spontaneous combustion between her and Wil in the massage room would stay between them. She moved past him to go into the dining room. "Bring some plates," she instructed. "And don't ever come here again without calling first." She walked out.

Michael smiled. He took instructions from his coach, but it stopped there. He followed her inside.

They spent the next half hour finishing up dessert with Michael regaling them with stories of the NBA. Barbara was getting an intense headache and her usually melt-in-your-mouth peach cobbler tasted like dry wood to her.

"So you met Ms. Barbara while you were in rehab?" Chauncey quizzed.

"Yep. She whipped me right into shape with those magic hands." He flashed that paparazzi smile at her, and Wil threw daggers. Her head pounded.

Barbara jumped up. "Let me take these plates into the kitchen. It's getting late." She tossed Michael a look.

He slowly stood up. "I really should be going." He turned to Wil. "Nice meeting you."

"Likewise." He stood up and shook Michael's hand and suddenly felt very old and out of shape.

"And you, young man, stay on the offense," he said, pointing a long finger in Chauncey's direction.

He grinned broadly. "Sure will."

Michael turned to Barbara. "Good to see you. Thanks for dessert." He leaned down and kissed her cheek.

"Sure." She dared not look at Wil.

"I can see myself out." He waved goodbye and walked out.

Barbara was suddenly exhausted. She felt as if she'd been up for hours, working in the fields. She wanted to collapse. That was the most emotionally draining hour she'd spent in ages.

Chauncey couldn't stop talking about Michael and what he was going to tell all his friends in school. Wil looked like he was going to explode.

Barbara reached out to touch him and he pulled away. He might as well have smacked her.

"I'm gonna get out of here, too. Busy day tomorrow."

"But tomorrow is your day off, isn't it?"

He went to the hall closet and took out his and Chauncey's coats. "C, come on, let's go."

"Are you going to ignore me?"

He looked at her. "Oh, you mean like you ignored me while your ex–boy toy was here?"

Her insides twisted. Heat rose to her face. "Ex–boy toy?" She snapped out the words and jerked her neck to the side. "Is that what you said?"

Wil put on his coat. "That's what he is, isn't he? Let's go, Chauncey!" He pulled the door open.

Chauncey pulled up. "Night, Ms. Barbara. Dinner was great. And meeting Michael Townsend…" He grinned.

Barbara forced her thoughts to clear and grabbed hold of her manners. She lightly patted his shoulders. "You're most welcome. Anytime."

Chauncey followed his father out. Barbara stood in the doorway until she heard the downstairs door slam shut. She winced. Slowly she closed the door and a sinking sensation settled in the pit of her stomach.

Chapter 9

Stephanie was in a dismal mood. She hadn't spoken to Tony in days and he hadn't tried to contact her, either. Maybe it was just as well, she concluded as she parked her BMW at an underground parking garage in the West Village. She had an appointment to meet Terri at Barnone. Although she knew it was one of Tony's favorite haunts, that hadn't been the deciding factor on a meeting spot. If she just so happened to run into him...well, so be it. The plan was to enjoy some downtime while talking business.

She walked up to the hostess at the podium and gave Terri's name.

"Right this way. Your party is already here."

Stephanie took in the artsy but sleek decor. It had the right amount of sophistication with an urban edge. The music was pumping but it wasn't overwhelming. You didn't have to scream to be heard. The main level was moderately full even for four in the afternoon.

The hostess led her to the mezzanine level and around several tables to a banquette located alongside the panoramic windows.

Terri waved when she saw Stephanie walking in her direction.

The hostess put two menus on either side of the table. "Your server will be right with you," she said.

"Nice spot," Stephanie said while sitting down.

"You have to come at night. The stars roll up in here like dice at a crapshoot, all trying to act like they don't want to be noticed but really do anyway."

"I can imagine." She stole a surreptitious look around wondering, possibly hoping to see Tony as she made herself comfortable.

"Their drinks are the best," Terri said, looking over the menu.

"I'm driving. So I have to go easy."

"I totally understand…but don't mind me." She laughed. "So how's everything going? You seem a bit distracted." She paused, craning her neck forward. "Steph?"

Stephanie focused on Terri. "Huh, sorry. What are you drinking?"

"That's not the last thing I said." She grinned sympathetically. "You okay?"

Stephanie let her guard down. Her shoulders slumped a bit. She rested her arms on the table and folded her hands. Terri was cool. She liked her a lot. They hadn't made a real leap from friends to confidantes, but she felt that she could trust Terri's judgment and it wouldn't be jaded from having known her for years like the girls.

"Man trouble," she began.

"You and Tony?"

"Let's say more me than Tony."

The server arrived to take their orders. Stephanie ordered a plate of chicken grilled tacos and a Cosmo. Terri decided on a seafood platter and a frozen piña colada minus the rum. Once the server was gone Stephanie told Terri about the falling-out she and Tony had over her not moving in with him.

Terri was silent for a moment once Stephanie was finished. The server returned with their drinks. "Your food will be out shortly." She hurried off.

Terri picked up her drink and took a sip. Stephanie was beginning to think that she'd made an awful mistake unloading her laundry. She reached for her drink and immediately wished she'd had the real thing.

Terri looked Stephanie straight in the eyes. "Do you love him?" she asked point-blank.

"I think I do. Sometimes." She wrapped her hands around the frosted goblet.

"Wrong answer. What is most important to you—right at this moment—your freedom or finally having someone who cares only about you?"

"Of course I want someone who only cares about me. But I don't feel I should have to give up something to get it."

Terri's right brow rose an inch. "That's what relationships are, Steph, give and take, sacrifices, thinking about someone before you think about yourself, wanting that person to be happy and wanting to be a part of that happiness."

Stephanie chortled. "Same thing Tony said."

"He said it because it's true. For real adult relationships to work, for love to work, both parties need to want the same thing…each other and no other."

The waitress arrived with their meals and set them down on the table. "Will there be anything else, ladies?"

"No, thanks," they said in unison.

Stephanie pushed her food around on her plate with her fork. "I don't know what it is," she said softly.

Terri looked across at her. "What *what* is?"

"Why it's so hard for me to really give myself to another person. My track record is miserable. I have a history of getting involved with people who are either physically or emotionally unavailable. I convince myself that it can work, turn a blind eye to all the warning signs, and then find some way to get out of it before they wake up and walk away from me."

"What are the warning signs with Tony?"

Stephanie put her folk down. "None."

"And that's more of a problem than anything else," she stated more than asked. "The only obstacle this time is you."

"He'll eventually leave, you know. They always do," Stephanie said as if it was gospel. "I may as well cut my losses now before I get in any deeper."

Terri frowned. "You honestly believe that?"

"Of course. Either by circumstance or design, they all leave."

"That's a pretty pessimistic viewpoint. What about all the couples that do make it, the ones that truly last until death do them part?"

"Those are the exceptions, not the rule." She chewed thoughtfully. "The major cause of divorce in this country is marriage."

"Girl, all jokes aside, you got issues." She gave a rueful smile.

"Probably," she conceded.

"So what are you going to do?"

She shrugged slightly. "I don't know. I guess if Tony decides he still wants to see me on my terms, then we can continue in this relationship. If not…"

"I think if you gave yourself and him half a chance, you'd be surprised how wonderful it is to love and be loved."

Stephanie looked at her. Chances were something she didn't take. She analyzed all the possibilities, weighed the odds, and came up with a plan. It was how she lived her life. She'd gotten this far. And she was happy. Wasn't she?

Barbara and Elizabeth were taking a well-deserved break in the café.

"So he just showed up?" Elizabeth snapped her fingers. "Without calling?"

Barbara nodded, then took a sip of her tea. "He was the absolute last person I expected to see on the other side of my door. Of course Chauncey was totally enamored of him and he rubbed Wil raw to no end."

"I can imagine."

"But that's not the worst of it."

"Worst?" Her brows rose.

Barbara set down her cup. "The entire time he was there was a battle of testosterone. It would have been funny had it been someone else's life in someone else's living room."

"What did Wil say?"

"He essentially accused me of coming on to Michael and ignoring him the entire time."

Elizabeth looked closely at her friend. She knew Barbara's past with Michael. They'd been engaged even though Barbara had some ambivalent feelings about their age difference. Barbara was the practical one of the quartet. She was the voice of reason in a storm. She'd totally stepped out of her comfort zone when she became involved with Michael. Going back to Wil was returning to the familiar, even though there'd been years in between since they'd been together. It was comfortable. Although Elizabeth knew that there had been some issues between Barbara and Michael, she often wondered if it wasn't some subconscious excuse to get out of a relationship that would challenge her on a level she wasn't familiar with.

"How right was Wil?" Elizabeth asked.

"What do you mean?"

"Was he right? Were you ignoring him?"

"N-no, of course not," she said without conviction. "If anything I was more in shock than in awe of Michael being there."

"How did you feel when you saw him again?"

"I—I didn't feel anything." She reached for her cup.

"Barb, this is me, your best friend."

Barbara sighed heavily. "All right, I admit, there were…some feelings there. But I put them right where they belonged—behind me." She thought for a moment how she had felt when Michael stood at the door, when he came up behind her in the kitchen, when he looked into her eyes. No, she hadn't forgotten the hot passion between them, the way he'd reawakened her sexuality, made her feel desirable again. Sure she'd felt that tingle, that heat run through her veins. But Michael was her past. Wil was her present and her future. At least she hoped so.

"All the reasons why I broke it off with Michael are still valid. He expected me to not have a life of my own if we married. He has a jealous streak and I know in my heart he'd want kids some day and that's something I can never give him. I don't have those issues with Wil."

"As long as you're sure," Elizabeth said.

"I am." She sipped her tea. Wasn't she?

Elizabeth studied her friend of more than

fifteen years. Barbara Allen was steady as they come. They'd shared so much together, joys, sorrows, triumphs, and defeats. Yet through it all Barbara had never wavered. So this was a first for Elizabeth, or rather a second, both instances involved Michael Townsend. He was the only entity in Barbara's life wherein she was caught sitting on the proverbial fence. The phenomenon was more curious than troubling. The question that plagued Elizabeth was, besides Michael's youth, what was it about him that rattled Barbara's rock-solid foundation?

Elizabeth leaned forward, drawing Barbara's complete attention. "Does Wil make you feel the same way that Michael did?"

"I don't know what you mean."

"Of course you do. You're stalling for an answer." She waited a beat. "You know you can be honest with me."

"I know," she said on a breath. "When I was with Michael…" Her eyes took on a faraway cast. "He reminded me that I was still a passionate, desirable woman. I never felt that way with Marvin. I mean, I loved my husband, but sex was…well, sex…pleasurable but nothing I'd

write an article about. And before I married
Marvin, the only other man I'd been with was
Wil.

"With Wil it was that young, intense, crazy
kinda sex, all the more exciting because of the
possibility of getting caught." She chuckled at
the memory of their many escapades.

Barbara folded her hands on top of the table.
"There have been a couple of men after Marvin,
both disastrous and best left unsaid. Then
Michael came into my life. I couldn't have been
more stunned if I'd found out I was America's
Next Top Model."

They both broke out in laughter. Then slowly
sobering, Barbara continued. "I'd never felt the
way Michael made me feel. *Never*. I didn't really
know the power of an orgasm until I had one with
him." She bit down on her bottom lip.

Elizabeth arched her brow in awe. She wanted
to ask why she'd left him, but held her tongue.

Barbara shrugged slightly. "But great sex isn't
everything. All the other pieces have to fit as
well."

"Is that how it is with Wil—all the pieces fit?"

Barbara offered a soft smile. "Yeah, they do.

And now that I know how to get and give what I want in bed it all works."

"Listen, you know more than anyone how much I want you to be happy, and as your friend I have the responsibility to be honest with you. I was there the day Wil walked into the spa. I saw the look on your face. And I'm sitting here right now and saw the look, not just on your face but in your eyes, when you talk about Michael. There's something still there, and if you truly plan on having a lasting relationship with Wil, then you really need to examine how you feel about Michael."

Barbara slowly shook her head in amazement. "This is the kind of craziness you're supposed to go through in your teens, your twenties, even early thirties, but damn, not at our age."

"Well, like the saying goes, men are like buses, there's another one coming right behind it. And just because we can catch a bus at a reduced fare doesn't mean we can't enjoy the ride!"

Barbara slapped her palm on the table and laughed. "You sho right about that. And with the reduced fare we have more money for more rides."

"Whew, girl, you need to stop."

"But you're right," Barbara admitted, regaining a serious tone. "I do need to come to terms with my feelings, squash all my doubts once and for all."

"You owe it to yourself, to Michael, and to Wil." She reached across the table and took Barbara's hands in hers. "You have two men who love you. And parts of you love both of them for different reasons. But one man deserves all of Barbara Allen. And you deserve to spend the rest of your life happy, not second-guessing your decisions."

"Thanks," Barbara said softly and squeezed Elizabeth's hands with affection. "You're always there for me."

"That's what friends are for."

"Speaking of friends, I've been kind of concerned about Stephanie. She acted so weird the other night at my house when we were talking about the guy you met through Ron." Barbara got up from the table, collected the cups and plates, then put them in the sink.

"Yeah." Elizabeth's expression pinched. "She's been pretty self-contained lately. Steph was always the outgoing, nonstop-talking party girl of the group. But lately she seems so different."

"I know. The couple of times I've run into her at the spa she's pleasant but distracted."

"Honestly, she hasn't been the same since that crazy man and his crazier wife started harassing her."

"I guess I would be on edge too if I was getting harassing phone calls and my married ex-lover pops up at my place of employment."

"You have a point there. I would have thought that with her finally settling down with Tony her anxiety would disappear."

Barbara turned from the sink, hand on hip, brow arched and knowing. "Now we both know that men and anxiety are one and the same—one way or the other."

Elizabeth let out a laugh. "Girl, you ain't nevah lie!" She got up from the table and stretched. "Well, since you chased Michael away and pissed off Wil, and Ron is going to hang out with his friend Ali, why don't we go to a movie later on after work? If it doesn't snow."

"Sounds good. That new movie with Terrance Howard is out."

"Works for me."

"Speaking of which, we need to get over to the spa and open up."

"Ah, yes, the drudgery of watching muscle-bound men, dripping in sex appeal and sweat, wearing formfitting T-shirts all day long. Humph, it really wears me out!"

Barbara chuckled. "Tough life we have, but somebody's gotta do it." She walked toward the front and got their coats from the closet. "With you doing all this man watching, how are things going with you and Ron?" She handed Elizabeth her coat.

"Couldn't be happier. I feel like I've been emancipated after damn near thirty years of marriage to Matthew."

"At least you can finally say his name," Barbara teased, referring to the time when he could only be referred to as "that bastard."

Elizabeth laughed lightly. "And do you know that for all the hell he put me through with that little hussy of an assistant of his, they aren't even together?"

"Get outta here." She closed the closet and put on her coat.

Elizabeth draped her scarf around her neck.

"Yep. He told the girls a couple of weeks ago when he stopped in the restaurant."

Barbara opened the door and they walked out. "At least he stays in touch with his children."

"For what it's worth," she groused.

"What would you do if Matt tried to come back to you?" She turned and locked her apartment door.

"Please don't even say the words. It's something I'd rather not entertain as a thought."

They headed down the hallway. "We really need to have breakfast together more often," Barbara said. "Gives us a chance to fill in all the gaps."

"And there's always something."

They stepped out into the biting air. "You got that right. There always is."

Chapter 10

Stephanie had just gotten off the phone with the phone company to have her number changed and was appalled at the hoops she had to jump through. The bottom line was if she was receiving annoying phone calls, they suggested buying a whistle and whistling into the phone each time the culprit called, keeping a logbook of the dates and times of the calls, and advising the caller that she would report them if they didn't stop. She almost laughed at the absurdity of it all. The truth of it was, the rep confessed, they were running out of phone numbers in her area, and if these measures didn't help in a month's time they would issue her a new number.

The only consolation was that she hadn't received any more calls from Marilyn in the past couple of weeks, but she hadn't received any calls from Tony, either.

She'd been so confident that he would have seen the light by now and called her. She supposed she could have called him as well. But that would have painted her as weak and not willing to stand by her convictions.

This was all so stupid, she thought, walking into her kitchen. She put two slices of bread in the toaster, then hunted around in the fridge for a container of yogurt.

If she was honest with herself she would admit how much she missed him. The things Terri had said to her the other day still rang in her head.

What was she so afraid of, and a bigger question, where did her fears of commitment stem from?

All of her friends seemed to have come to terms with their lives, loves, and expectations.

They'd found that place inside themselves where they could allow someone else to cohabit. Why couldn't she? What was wrong with her?

She was strong, intelligent, good-looking, terribly afraid, and very alone.

You're not alone, she heard Tony say. *I'm here for you if you let me.*

The toast popped. She stared at it for a moment, then abruptly walked out of the kitchen.

It was barely nine in the morning. If Tony's schedule hadn't changed dramatically in the past couple of weeks, he should still be home. She grabbed her coat and purse and hurried out.

It took her twenty minutes to get to Lower Manhattan and another fifteen to find a parking space where she felt reasonably comfortable that she wouldn't get a ticket or, worse, towed.

It had begun to rain while she was en route, an icy rain that went right through your bones. From the looks of things between swats from her windshield wipers, the icy rain was turning to icy slush. She peered over into the backseat hoping she'd stashed her umbrella on the floor. When she leaned over the seat to get it, she noticed a couple coming out of Tony's building huddled together under a huge black umbrella.

She almost ignored them before she realized that the man with his arm around the woman was Tony. The woman looked up at him with a smile on her face. He leaned down and picked the little girl up into his arms and hugged her tight. Stephanie felt paralyzed.

The trio walked to an SUV parked a few feet from his building. Tony opened the passenger door for the woman, strapped the little girl into a booster seat in the back, then ran around the front and got behind the wheel of the car. They drove off, but were stopped at the corner for a red light.

Stephanie finally found her senses and jumped out of her car into the middle of the wet street, nearly losing her footing on the slippery asphalt. *Well, what are you going to do, silly, stand here or run them down?* The rain and ice came faster. In seconds she was drenched.

The SUV started to pull off. *It had Connecticut plates.*

Stephanie hurried back to her car to write the number down before she forgot. As she did, a million thoughts ran through her head: Who was that woman and little girl with Tony and what was she going to do with the license plate number?

She stared at the number scrawled on the back of an envelope. Water from her hair dripped onto it. She pushed her soaking hair away from her face. *Connecticut.* Why hadn't she gotten out of the car when she recognized him? Because she'd done what millions of women have done for ages—freeze. Now he could always come back and say, "It wasn't me." Maybe it wasn't. Maybe it was just someone who looked like him. After all, she was on the other side of the street. Her range of vision was hampered by the weather.

That was probably it. She was being silly, looking for trouble where there wasn't any. She took a brush from her purse and brushed her wet hair back into a ponytail and held it together with a rubber band that she'd found in the glove compartment. She checked her makeup in the rearview mirror, then added a dash more lipstick.

All this foolishness and the mind games she was playing with herself would be squashed when she rang Tony's bell. He was probably upstairs fixing one of his fabulous breakfasts. She grabbed her umbrella and her purse and got out. The instant she put her foot down in the icy mess she wished she'd worn her boots instead of loafers as if it were June instead of February.

She crossed the street as quickly as she could and ducked into his building, sidestepping a teen who had every inch of her ear pierced and adorned and a hoop earring through her nose. Her mother would have killed her, she thought absently as she walked to the bank of doorbells in the foyer.

She quickly scrolled the list and located T. Dixon, 8B. Tony lived in one of those humongous prewar buildings that had two sides—the odd and the even. She pressed the bell and waited, rehearsing her little speech in her head.

No answer. Her stomach jerked.

He had to be there. She pressed the bell again. No answer.

Slowly she turned from the bank of names and numbers just as someone was coming out. She quickly turned around and hurried inside before the door shut.

Probably in the shower, she told herself as

she crossed the black and white marble floor to the elevator. *Didn't hear the bell, that's all.*

The elevator arrived, she stepped on, pressed 8, and waited, thankful that there was no one else on board with whom she'd feel compelled to either make small talk with or ignore.

The doors opened. She stepped out and turned right. His apartment was at the end of the hall. She drew in a breath, raised her hand, and knocked. She waited and listened closely for any signs of life.

Nothing.

She pulled her cell phone from her purse and dialed his home number. She listened to the phone ring and ring from inside until his voice came through on the answering machine. She didn't bother to leave a message, and all the ugly thoughts she didn't want to think about rushed to the surface.

It was Tony she'd seen getting into that SUV with a woman and a child.

Stephanie looked at the door one last time, then headed back to the elevator. Before she got on she called his cell phone. His voice mail was her answer. She didn't bother to leave a message there, either. What was the point?

She returned to her car. The icy rain had turned to a driving snow. She didn't even notice as she made her way across the street.

Mindlessly she got behind the wheel. For several moments she simply sat there, the world around her growing dimmer, blanketed in white. By rote she turned on the car, the heat, the windshield wipers.

This is what she got, she concluded as she put the car in gear. The minute she was ready to let down her guard...

Her throat constricted. She wouldn't cry. She wouldn't. But she did anyway.

Chapter 11

"It's really coming down out here," Ron said, pulling his coat collar up around his neck.

"They said a 'chance' of snow," Ali said, as they exited the pool hall. "But I swear the weathermen don't know any more than the aches in my knees."

Ron chuckled. "You got that right." He stuck his hands in thick black leather gloves. "Hungry?"

"Starved."

"Wanna go over to Delectables?"

"Sure. Food's good and the service is better. I'll follow you in my car."

"I'm parked down the street. See you there." He hunched his shoulders against the wind and trudged down the block.

"Man, it feels good in here," Ali said, stomping his feet on the welcome mat once he got inside the restaurant.

Ron snatched his wool watchman cap from his head and brushed snow off his wide shoulders. "You would think with weather like this the place would be empty."

Delectables had two medium-sized rooms with about eight tables in each section as well as counter seating for five. From what Ron could tell, there were maybe three available tables in the whole place.

"Well, hello." Dawne walked over and pecked Ron on the cheek, then turned to Ali. "Good to see you again." She put her hands on narrow hips. "You guys picked a great day to come out and play."

"Looks like a lot of other people thought the same thing," Ali said.

"I know. It's so weird, nice weather and folks trickle in. Blizzard and we can barely keep up with the orders." She shrugged her right shoulder. "New Yorkers. Go figure."

"Do you have help?" Ron asked, wondering how only she and her twin sister, Desiree, could manage.

"Oh yeah. We hired two part-time waitresses who come in whenever we need extra help and we have two cooks." She laughed lightly. "Our part-time help has become more full-time since Desi and I have been supplying the food for the spa. But it's all good. So." She clapped her hands together. "Can I get you a table or something to go?"

Ron hooked his thumb over his shoulder toward the door. "I'm in no hurry to go back out there."

Dawne grinned. "Follow me." She snatched up two menus from the rack and led them to a vacant table at the far side of the counter in the front room.

Once they were seated and had placed their orders, Ron asked Ali how his apartment hunting was going.

"Slow. Seen plenty of great places, but these

New York prices are highway robbery." He shook his head in disgust. "They really don't want us here anyway," he said, easily slipping into his militant stance. "And one way to ensure that is to price us out of the market."

"The powers that be will never admit that, though. I see it every day in the construction business. One neighborhood after another being 'revitalized.'"

"That's the code word for homogenized—all the color and vitality and culture drained out."

Ron bobbed his head in agreement. "Exactly." He glanced toward the door when it opened. "There's one of the fabulous foursome."

Ali looked over his shoulder and his stomach knotted.

Stephanie walked up to the counter without seeing them. Ron got up and walked over to her.

"Hey, Steph. Picked a bad day to go out and play."

She turned, looked at him with dull eyes, and forced a smile. "Hi, Ron. Figured I'd grab something and head home."

He looked at her more closely. "You okay?"

"Yeah, fine. Just cold."

"You're welcome to join us." He glanced over his shoulder toward Ali.

Stephanie followed his movement. A moment of recollection darted around in her head. She blinked, looked again.

"He's a friend of yours?"

"Yeah, why?"

"I'd swear he was the same man who kept me from falling on my behind a few days ago."

"Could be. He's the kind of guy who wouldn't let a woman fall on her behind—if he could help it," he added with a grin.

Maybe some company right now would be a good thing, she thought. The idea of sitting alone in her apartment was becoming a more unappealing notion with each tick of the clock.

"If you're sure you don't mind."

"Of course not. Come on."

She followed him to the table. The low buzz of conversation, soft music playing from some hidden source, mixed with the tantalizing aromas of tempting food all made the chill that had permeated her bones slowly begin to thaw. She unbuttoned her three-quarter navy blue car coat, then extended her hand.

"I do believe we've met before."

Ali rose, standing a full head above her five-foot-nine body. This time Stephanie got a good look at her knight in shining armor. Not only was he tall but he was built like a football player—broad muscular shoulders and arms that were clearly visible beneath the fitted knit shirt. His hands were large but gentle as he shook hers, but the palms were rough, testifying to a man who worked hard for his money. His head was bald and he had a warm chestnut complexion with dark wide eyes and thick brows. Upon first look one would think he was much younger than he was. But she could tell that this was a mature man, much older than her from the lines of experience around his mouth and the depth of it in his eyes.

Something flickered in his eyes, ticked in his left cheek. His smile was broad and inviting.

"Oh yes, on the sidewalk."

"That's me. You saved me from much pain and embarrassment."

"Anytime." He released her hand and quickly came around to pull out and hold her chair as she sat down.

"At least let me make formal introductions," Ron interrupted. "Stephanie Moore, this is Ali Aziz."

Stephanie's eyes widened. "You're the Ali that Elizabeth told us about. You were a Black Panther."

"Word gets around." He chuckled and returned to his seat. "Yes, I was and still am at heart. I was one of the founding members of the Atlanta Chapter, which is where I met this guy when he was no more than a kid." He chucked Ron in the arm.

"That is so incredible. We could sure use some Black Panthers today," she said, pulling her chair closer to the table. She shrugged off her coat and let it fall over the back of the chair and inadvertently caught an unguarded expression on Ali's face. The guileless look that coats your countenance when you think no one is watching. A jolt of something snapped inside her. Her heart hammered for an instant and then slowed.

"Hey, Ms. Stephanie. I didn't see you come in," Dawne said.

Stephanie gave her head a short sharp shake

to dispel the funny feeling she had, then looked up at Dawne. "Yeah, I kinda slid in. Busy evening?"

"Very. Can I get you something?"

"Your fabulous vegetable soup would be perfect."

"Large or small?"

"Large."

"Coming right up. Yours will be out shortly," she said to Ron and Ali.

"What brings you out in all this weather?" Ron asked.

Stephanie's thoughts shifted back the original reason she'd come out in the first place—to make up with Tony. She focused on the smoothie menu. "Wasn't anything like this when I came out," she said sideways, avoiding his question. "What about you two?"

"We were getting our pool game on," Ali said. "Came outside and…" He extended his large hand toward the window that was now frosted with snow and ice.

"A real mess," Stephanie murmured. She gazed at Ali. "You seem so familiar to me, and not from the other day." Her expression creased as she tried to place him. "I can't think where I know you from."

He shifted a bit in his seat. "I guess I have one of those faces. They say everyone has a twin."

"Hmm." She shrugged it off. "So you and Ron work together?"

"Yeah, my old buddy put me on the team." He patted Ron on the back.

"How long have you been in New York?"

"A couple of months. I was in Chicago for a while, then L.A., Florida. Got tired of the hurricanes so I came here."

"He's being modest. He failed to mention that during his travels he was responsible for setting up mentoring programs for troubled kids in all of those cities."

Ali looked mildly embarrassed.

"That is impressive. How many programs do you have in place?"

"Eight that I manage."

"You should be so proud."

"It's the least I can do. There are so many kids out there just drifting with nothing in their futures but trouble or worse."

"Ever think about starting something here?"

Stephanie asked, totally fascinated. There was a special place in her heart for anyone who reached out to those less fortunate, especially kids.

"Actually I have. Not sure yet how I will go about it."

"I'd love to help if I could."

"I'll definitely keep that in mind."

Ron snapped his fingers. "Not to change the subject but maybe you can help. Ali's been looking for a place. You think Ann Marie might be able to help him find something?"

"I don't see why not. I'll ask her. Are you looking to buy or rent?"

"Rent for the time being. I like my freedom. Not sure if I want to tie myself to a house."

"I'll have Ann Marie give you a call. What's your number?" She took out her Axim and put in his number as he dictated it.

"I really appreciate that."

She stuck the PDA back in her purse. "No problem. If Ann Marie can't find you something, there's nothing to be found. She's like a blood-hound when it comes to locating property."

A waitress arrived with their orders. "Will there be anything else?"

They all said no.

"Ron tells me you're part of the fabulous foursome."

Stephanie giggled. "Oh, we have a name?"

"What's your role?"

"I'm the publicist."

"Stephanie was responsible for getting the spa some major news coverage. Now she has her own business."

Ali looked into her eyes and smiled. "That's wonderful. Congratulations," he said in a quiet voice. "Running your own business takes a lot of hard work."

"No harder than what you do. I can only imagine the number of lives you've changed. I try to stay on top of things—it's the publicist in me. But I have to admit I've never heard your name mentioned or seen any write-ups about your work."

"I try to keep a low profile, stay behind the scenes, not out front. It's not about me, but about the kids."

She took a sip of her soup. "I'd like to hear more about it—the behind-the-scenes look."

"Okay." He took a bite of his veggie burger

and chewed thoughtfully. "I guess the idea came to me…"

He talked about how he saw so many aimless young men in his neighborhood with nothing on their minds and no future on the horizon. And how things for young black Americans had deteriorated since the height of the Civil Rights movement. He knew he couldn't resurrect the Panthers, but he could use what he'd learned about discipline and self-respect to the kids. He called on a few friends and they started hanging on the street corners and in the parks talking to the young boys. Before they knew it there was a regular group that would get together in the park twice a week, and the numbers kept growing. He and his friends put their money together and rented a storefront. They'd bring different speakers in to talk to them about life, sex, drugs, education, and the opportunities available to them. One storefront led to another and another.

"Amazing," she said. "Do you work with young girls?"

He nodded. "We just started working with young girls about a year ago in Florida. We need more women volunteers, but it's coming together."

"Like I said, if you ever decide to bring your

program to New York I'd be willing to help."
She finished off her soup and wiped her mouth
with the paper napkin. "This has been great. Just
what I needed on a day like today. But…" She
pushed back from the table. "I need to get home."
She reached in her purse for her wallet.

Ali held up his hand. "Don't worry about it."

"Are you sure?"

"Aw, go on," Ron said, "between two hardworking men we can handle a bowl of soup."

She laughed. "Correction, large bowl. Thanks."
She extended her hand to Ali. "It was really nice
to officially meet you."

He held her hand, a soft smile on his lips.
"The pleasure was mine."

Her eyes ran over his face and she felt an odd
sense of comfort. She turned her attention to
Ron. "Always good seeing you. Make sure you
keep our girl happy."

He pressed his hand to his chest. "That's the
most important job I have."

Stephanie chuckled and put on her coat.

"I'll walk you to your car," Ali offered.

"I'll be fine. And I promise I won't fall.
Good night."

"Night," they said in unison.

Ali watched her leave, then slowly sat down in his seat.

"You okay?" Ron asked. "You have this dazed look in your eyes."

Ali ducked his head to hide his embarrassment. "Just thinking, that's all."

Ron looked toward the door. "She's a little young for you if that's what you're thinking."

Ali hesitated for a moment. "Look, there's something I want to tell you. But you gotta swear you won't say anything. Not now, maybe never."

Chapter 12

The moment Stephanie entered her empty apartment the events of earlier in the day came rushing back with a vengeance.

Tony and another woman—and a child. She took off her coat and hung it on the shower rod in the bathroom. She still couldn't believe it, or rather she didn't want to believe it.

How could he have professed loving her, wanting her to move in with him when he was obviously involved with someone else? Was the child his? A physical pain gripped her insides at the thought.

It was over. Plain and simple. She went into her bedroom, tossed her purse on the bed, and got out of her clothes. Suddenly bone weary, she sat down on the side of the bed. She reached for her bag, took out her phone, and put it on the nightstand with the intention of charging it before she turned in for the night.

She flopped back on the bed in her underwear and stared up at the ceiling. She'd get over this just like she'd gotten over every other hurdle and disappointment in her life. One day at a time. She had more important things to worry about besides feeling sorry for herself.

Good riddance, Anthony Dixon. She got under the covers and turned out the light. Tomorrow was another day and she intended to start it off feeling a helluva lot better than she did at the moment.

When Stephanie awoke the following morning she was alarmed to realize that it was still snowing. She tossed off her teal blue down comforter and put her feet down on the wood floor. She flinched from the cold that slapped the bottoms of her feet.

Bending over she peeked under the dust ruffle for her slippers. Shoving her feet into her Lugs, she walked over to the window.

Nothing was moving. Cars parked on the street looked like rows of igloos on a residential block in Alaska.

Briskly she rubbed her arms as the numbing chill begged to get inside her comfy bedroom. Jeez, the weatherman didn't know jack. All that fancy equipment and they couldn't predict a major freaking snowstorm.

She turned away, annoyed. There was no doubt that she was pretty much grounded for the day. From the looks of things outside, the plows hadn't even come through her street yet.

She went off to the kitchen and took out her favorite ginger and honey tea and put on a kettle of water to boil while she got herself together in the bathroom.

By the time she'd cleaned the sleep from her eyes and brushed her teeth until they gleamed, she heard the kettle whistle.

As she poured the boiling water over the

teabag in the cup she wondered what she was going to do with herself all day, and more important, what was she going to eat? To say her cupboards were bare was an understatement. Looking at Stephanie's kitchen, one would think that she loved to cook. Her kitchen was state-of-the-art with every kind of utensil imaginable. Stainless steel pots hung from a ceiling rack that matched the stainless steel freezer and built-in range. All of which were merely attractions for the eye but sparked no desire in her to learn her way around the kitchen.

She pulled open the fridge hoping to perhaps find a carton of Chinese food that she could warm up in the microwave. But all she saw was a half carton of half-and-half and the Tupperware of leftover soup that she and Tony had shared.

She pushed the door shut. Was he still with that woman? Why should she give a damn? She'd wanted out of the relationship anyway. It was stupid of her to pop up at his apartment like she'd done. Stupid to think… Who was she? Was that their child? How could he not have told her?

"Agggh. I'm not going to make myself crazy. I'm not!"

She poured her cup of tea and took it to the living room, sat down on the love seat, then turned on her thirty-two-inch plasma television. It was another treat to herself after landing a successful account while she'd worked for Conrad at H. L. Reuben.

That was one of the things she missed about working for a large corporation—the perks. While she'd been employed she had an expense account, annual bonuses, a hefty commission on top of her high five-figure salary. All those perks and the solid cash base had all helped to cover Samantha's care. She knew she'd worked hard, she had to. It was the major reason why she became involved with Conrad in the first place and why she continued the affair. Her relationship with him guaranteed her the financial security she needed to care for Samantha, and that was more important than anything else. No matter what the cost to herself.

She finished off her tea and set the cup in the sink. But that didn't make it right, she admitted. There should never be a "good reason" why one had an affair with someone who was married. What goes around comes around, she thought as she wandered back into her bedroom. Now she was seeing how it felt to have someone you loved be with someone else.

She stopped short. Her heart jerked in her chest. *Love?* Who the hell was in love? She shook her head. Even if it were possible for her it was over now.

"I need to get ready to head back to the city," Tony said to Leslie.

He'd spent the past two days at his sister's home in New Haven and they'd talked like they hadn't in a very long time. He told her all about Stephanie and how much he loved her, that she was the first woman to claim his heart since Kim when he thought that loving again was impossible. He told her about his invitation to come and live with him and her reaction. Leslie's advice was to give Stephanie some time, and just as he had his reasons for living his life the way he did, Stephanie surely had her reasons as well. Instead of going off half-cocked, what they needed to do was talk— honestly—about their hopes and their fears.

Leslie put the frying pan in the sink and ran hot water over it, then turned to her brother. "It's been great having you here." She wiped her hands on a yellow-and-white-checkered dish towel. "Especially for Joy."

He nodded slowly. "It's been good for me too. I never realize how much I miss her until I see her again."

Leslie leaned back against the edge of the sink. "She really needs you, Tony." Her eyes implored him.

He turned away, crossed the room, and sat down at the kitchen table. "I know it's hard for you to understand, for anyone to understand. Every time I look at Joy I see Kim. And I know that her not being here is my fault, that Joy not having a mother is my fault." He shook his head vigorously. "The guilt eats away at me." His voice broke. "And even more so when I see Joy."

"Tony." She crossed the room and sat down opposite him. "It wasn't your fault. You have to believe that."

"Then whose fault is it?" he snapped at her. "I knew Kim should never have gotten pregnant. The doctors said it could kill her. But I let it happen and then I let her go through with it anyway—knowing the risks."

"But Kim knew the risks, too. She loved you and wanted to give you her love, and the result was Joy. You didn't trick her into getting pregnant. Besides, there was no guarantee that she would go into crisis during delivery." She lowered her gaze. "But she did."

"The doctors said it was possible—very possible. The strain of labor could easily set off a sickle cell crisis."

That day in the hospital bloomed before him. Kim had been getting weaker with each passing day. During the last four months of her pregnancy she'd had three major episodes that put her in the hospital. The baby was in danger and the doctors wanted to do a C-section. But the risks of delivery too early were just as high as waiting it out as long as possible.

"Maybe we should let them do the operation," he'd said to her as he held her hand. He pulled his chair closer to the hospital bed.

She shook her head. "No. They've said the baby is very small. She's already struggling. I want to give her a chance, Tony. Please."

"I don't want to lose you, Kim. I swear I don't think I can—"

"Shh, don't. We're going to get through this. I want to spend the rest of my life with you and our child." She smiled weakly. "It's what I want."

He brought her hand to his lips and kissed it, willing his strength to flow through her veins. He would do anything on earth to stop her pain, stop the suffering and the agony he'd witnessed her go through. He rested his head on the side of her bed while she stroked his hair. It was one of the many favorite things she did. He loved the feel of her tiny hands on him. They were incredibly soft and gentle from the very first time they'd met.

She was a cashier at a Barnes and Noble bookstore on Fourteenth Street in the Village. He'd walked in one evening after a photo shoot when he'd spotted a poster in the window announcing that James Patterson was doing a book signing. When he went inside, the store was packed. He couldn't get anywhere near one of his favorite authors. So he'd decided to walk around and see if he could find something to read. He was in the mystery aisle scanning the shelves.

"Can I help you find something?"

The voice sounded like it came from one of heaven's angels. When he turned she was smiling up at him. She was what would certainly be considered tiny. She stood no more than five feet five, and if she weighed more than one hundred pounds it would be a miracle. Her skin was the color of sautéed butter, thick black lashes framed wide doe-shaped eyes the color of midnight, her cheekbones were the kind that you dream of, and her mouth was so rich and lush you wanted to sink onto the soft pillows of her lips. Her inky dark hair hung to the middle of her back, and he could imagine it fanning out around her as she lay beneath him on his bed. He was totally mesmerized and for a moment couldn't speak.

She angled her head to the side. "Did you find what you were looking for?" she asked.

He ran his tongue across his suddenly dry lips. "Uh…just browsing."

"Okay. Enjoy." She turned to leave.

"Wait!" he said much too loud.

"Yes?" Curiosity danced in the darkness of her gaze.

"Uh, maybe you could suggest something."

She returned to his side and the soft scent of her, nearly undetectable, floated gently around her and enveloped him.

"What are you interested in?"

"A good mystery. Love figuring things out." He slid his hands into his pockets to keep from shifting a strand of her silken hair away from her face.

She turned toward the shelves and put her finger to her lips as she scanned the volumes, and Tony wished he were that finger. She reached for a book but wasn't quite able to get to it. Tony leaned toward her.

"This one?" he asked and his hand brushed hers. A shock rushed through his veins.

They both felt it. Her eyes snapped toward him. They laughed. The tension dispelled.

"Yes, that's the one. It just came in."

He took the book down from the shelf. "If you say it's good, I'll go with it."

She stared at him as if she wanted to say something, but didn't.

"Are you a mystery buff?"

Her smile was shy. "Horror and sci-fi."

His brow rose and a slow grin stretched his mouth. "I'm impressed. I figured you go for romance."

Her eyes raked him up and down. "Nothing wrong with a little romance."

"Touché. Anything you can recommend in that department?"

"Excuse me, miss, do you work here?"

Kim turned to the woman who'd come up behind her. "Yes, how can I help you?"

"I'm looking for a book for my teenage son. He needs it for a school report." She handed Kim a list.

Kim turned to Tony. "If there's anything else I can help you with let me know."

He lifted his chin in acknowledgment and watched her walk away. Damn, he felt like he'd been hit by lightning. He couldn't remember a woman having that kind of affect on him so suddenly. He gripped the book she'd given him. He had to see her again, find out who she was and everything about her.

Tony wound his way around the crowd that was beginning to disperse after the Patterson signing, and it was akin to running the gauntlet. He thought he caught a glimpse of her tiny form, but like mist she seemed to vanish.

He decided to come back the next day only to discover that she wasn't there. He tried every day for a week, and then like magic she was standing right next to him in Starbucks.

"Hi."

He couldn't believe his eyes. She was like an apparition. The urge to sweep her up in his arms and whisk her away was so overpowering that his temples began to pound.

"Hi. I…came back to look for you."

She looked uncomfortable for a moment. "Yeah, I was out for a few days." She glanced around. "Are you staying or going?"

"Staying, if you are."

"I have an hour. I'm on my lunch break."

"Then I'm staying."

They made their purchases and found a table in the back. They talked for more than an hour as if they had to squeeze in as much as they possibly could. The conversation was so easy, so light and insightful. She was a graduate student at Columbia working on her journalism degree and only worked part-time at the bookstore. She had a roommate, her best friend, Gwynne, who was a writer. She loved books and music and gourmet cooking. She had an infectious laugh and an internal warmth that reached out and embraced you like an old friend.

The hour went far too quickly, but they made

a date to see each other that night and they never looked back.

It was maybe two months into the relationship when Tony experienced firsthand what Kim endured during a crisis. The wait in the emergency room was pure torture. He'd always heard of sickle cell disease and its predominance in the African-American community. But he knew no one who had it and he certainly had never witnessed an episode. The physical pain that Kim was in was unbearable to watch. He felt useless, unable to do anything to alleviate her agony.

When the doctors finally came out they told him that she was resting and that they were going to keep her overnight, and since there was nothing more he could do, the doctor suggested that he go home.

Reluctantly he left and on his way out he was nearly run over by a woman whose countenance looked as if it were carved from the great totem poles of the American Indian. She was regal and the spitting image of what Kim would look like when she got older.

"Are you Mrs. Littlejohn?"

She stopped suddenly, her eyes wide with

something resembling fear. "Yes, yes." She pressed her palm to her breast. "Kim, is she all right?"

"Yes, the doctors said she's resting. But they are going to keep her overnight."

She seemed to shrink in relief as if the anxiety over her daughter was the starch in her back. Then she actually focused on Tony.

"You are the young man she talks about." Her smile didn't quite reach her eyes.

"Anthony Dixon."

"I'm glad that you were there for my daughter."

"So am I. And I plan to be for a long time."

"I hope you are a strong man. You will need it." With that she walked away.

Tony didn't realize just how strong he had to be. Between Kim's chronic episodes and stays in the hospital and her mother's blatant dislike for him, it was a hard road for him and Kim, but they endured. And against her mother's wishes, they married three years later.

Kim desperately wanted a child. The doctors all said no. She suffered two miscarriages that nearly killed her not only physically but spiritually as well. Tony said no more. He would not risk losing her. But in one careless night of passion she became pregnant again. This time she made it past the first trimester and they both became hopeful. The doctors were optimistic at first, but then the crises began, one after another, and then…she was gone. Her mother blamed him, cursed him for taking away her only child. And he swore to this day that the heartache of losing Kim was what eventually killed her mother. How could he not feel the weight of that kind of guilt?

"Daddy, Daddy, look what I drew."

He blinked, shook his head slightly, and focused on his daughter, the past receding to that hidden place in his heart. He took the drawing and smiled. It was a stick-figure picture of a little girl holding the hand of a man.

"That's me." She pointed to the little girl. "And that's you." She grinned, displaying the gap in her front teeth.

Tony's heart surged and he was suddenly overwhelmed with emotion. This was his baby, his and Kim's gift to the world. He owed it to both of them to do right.

He scooped her up and onto his lap. "You're very talented, you know." He kissed the top of her head.

She bobbed her head. "I know."

Leslie laughed. "And modest too."

Joy hopped down. "I'm going to make another one that you can take with you when you go."

Before Tony could react she'd run off into the next room. He looked up at his sister, who was still standing by the sink.

"I'm going to talk to Stephanie and tell her everything. And no matter how things turn out, I'm going to start being a real father to Joy."

"It's what Kim would have wanted, Tony."

His nostrils flared and his eyes filled. "I know. I know."

Chapter 13

Bored senseless, Stephanie puttered around the house rearranging things that didn't need to be rearranged. She watched the soaps for a while and then a few of the court shows until she couldn't take it anymore.

She wandered into her bedroom and took her PDA out of her purse to check her to do list and any upcoming appointments, which is when she remembered that she'd taken Ali's phone number and had promised to give it to Ann Marie.

She still couldn't shake the feeling that she

knew him. It was odd. There was no real recollection but more of a feeling of familiarity like
a favorite blanket. Strange. She shrugged it off
and pulled up his information. She glanced at the
digital clock on her nightstand. It was after two.
Ann Marie should be up and about. She didn't
imagine that she'd gone into work.

Stephanie reached for the phone and dialed
Ann Marie's number.

The phone rang and rang and she was just
about to hang up without leaving a message
when Ann Marie answered the phone, her voice
soft and husky.

"Girl, I know you are not still in the bed."

"Chile, when ya got a man like mine, no
reason to get out." She laughed wickedly.

"You are too much."

Ann Marie yawned loudly. "What's going on?
That man of yours should be keepin' ya warm on
a day like today."

"It's over."

"Say what?"

"Yeah."

"Hold on."

Stephanie heard some shuffling around and

low murmured voices, and then Ann Marie came back on the phone.

"I had to excuse myself so I can listen to this uninterrupted. What happened?" she asked. "Oh, hang on again."

Stephanie heard Ann Marie and her husband, Sterling, talking in the background.

"Sorry," Ann Marie apologized. "Sterling is suddenly feeling abandoned and decided to finally go and dig out the car. Now, back to you. Let me hear it."

Stephanie sighed heavily. "I really don't want to talk about it."

"Ya betta won talk 'bout sum'ting when ya get me out me bed and chased me man out de house," she chastised, her accent locked and loaded.

With great reluctance Stephanie relayed what had transpired up to and including her visit to his apartment and everything in between.

"Dayum." Ann Marie was thoughtful for a moment. "But she could have been anyone. Maybe a relative."

"Which I'm sure that's what he'll tell me. I was so stupid for not saying something when I saw them together. There would have been no way to fabricate a story," she said with disgust.

"That's true. Well, are you going to talk to him?"

"Why bother? I'm sure he'll only lie."

"Listen, no matter what you decide to do, for your own peace of mind you should settle it. I can tell you, it will haunt you forever if you just walk away with it hanging in the air."

"I just can't...I don't think I could bear it if he lied to me. You didn't see them together. There was love in his eyes."

"What if you could find out who the woman was before you spoke to him?"

"What do you mean?"

"You said you got the plate number."

"Yeah...What are you getting at?"

"Sterling is a lawyer. He has plenty of contacts in the police department. I'm sure he can get someone to run the plates."

A knot of apprehension twisted inside her. Run her plates? That was like spying. "Ann, I don't know."

"You have nothing to lose. At the worst, you'll find out who she is. The bottom line is, you must talk to him, whether you say it's over or not. It obviously wasn't or you wouldn't have gone over there. And if it really was you wouldn't care one way or the damned other."

Stephanie knew she was right. By nature she was a stickler for details. It's what made her stellar at her job. She never let details go unattended, and agenda items not in place and taken care of drove her crazy. If she didn't put some closure to this thing with her and Tony and get the answers that she needed, yes, it would haunt her forever.

"Okay," she relented, though the nature of what she was about to do did bug her. She gave Ann Marie the license plate number.

"Connecticut, huh? Well, I'll give it to Sterling when he gets back. As soon as he finds out something I'll let you know."

"Thanks, Ann...I think." She chuckled without a stitch of humor.

"Well, let me get myself together." She walked to the window and peeked out between the slats in the blinds. She spotted Sterling on the street shoveling snow along with about four other intrepid souls. "At least it stopped snowing.

One thing I always hated about the States was the cold-ass winters. If it wasn't for that no-good ex-husband of mine I would spend my winters in Jamaica." She sucked her teeth.

"Did he win the election?"

"Me don't know and don't care. I'm sure he told Raquel, but she knows better than to speak her pop's name to me after what he did."

Ann Marie had been through it with her very estranged husband, Terrance Bishop. He came back into her life after more than twenty years claiming to want her back only to find out that he simply wanted the perfect family picture for political purposes back in Jamaica. She'd nearly lost Sterling as a result.

"Oh, I almost forgot why I really called."

"There's more?"

She told him about Ron's friend Ali, who was looking for an apartment.

"Not a problem." She took down his number. "I'll give him a call. So, what's he like? Is he dangerous?" she asked in a teasing tone after Elizabeth had told them that he had been in jail.

"Actually, he seems anything but dangerous.

He's really nice. He feels like someone I've always known."

"Well, if you give him your seal of approval I will definitely find him something good."

"Thanks."

"Like I said, I'll call you when I find out something."

"Okay," she said on a breath.

"And hear me now. Don't be listening to no damned slow sad songs. Turn on some reggae and shake your boom-boom. You'll feel betta."

"Ann, you are too crazy. I'll talk to you later."

Ann giggled. "Bye."

Stephanie hung up the phone and felt mildly better. There was something a little underhanded about investigating someone without their knowledge. But if she got the information, at least she would know who and what she was dealing with.

While Sterling was out playing in the snow, Ann Marie took a quick shower, used her favorite body oil, and slipped into a brand-new Victoria's Secret catsuit and waited on the couch for Sterling to return. She wanted to make sure she buttered him up good and proper to ensure that he would do her this one little favor.

"Whoa, now this is what a man likes to come home to," Sterling said, a lecherous grin tugging at his mouth.

Ann Marie waved a slender finger. "Good things come to those who wait. I ran you a hot bath. Don't want those muscles to get stiff from the cold and all that shoveling."

He took off his coat and hung it on the rack by the door, then came fully into the living room. He walked up to her and leaned down until he was inches from her mouth. He tilted up her chin with the tip of his finger. "You're going to kill me, woman," he whispered harshly against her mouth.

"But you'll die a happy man."

"Promises, promises." He kissed her softly, then headed off to the steamy bath, taking off his shirt in the process.

Ann Marie watched the muscles in his back stretch and ripple and couldn't wait to run her hands all over them.

When Sterling emerged from the bathroom with no more on than a towel wrapped around his waist, Ann Marie almost forgot the plan. He came over to her.

"Now, where were we?" He stroked her shoulder and let his fingers drift over her breast.

She drew in a breath and forced herself to concentrate on the matter at hand. She took hold of his fingers and brought them to her lips. She slipped one in her mouth and slowly sucked on it.

Sterling dropped down in the space next to her, leaning forward to take a long overdue kiss.

She pressed her finger to his lips, then ran a nail down the center of his chest.

"I need you to do something for me."

He licked her finger. "Whatever you want." He ran his hand along her thigh.

"Good." Her hand traveled lower, settled on his belly for a moment, then journeyed downward to the thick bulge protruding in the towel. She cupped him and gave a gentle squeeze. Sterling groaned deep in his throat. "I need you to make a call for me. Find out about a license plate number."

"Hmm," he murmured, transported by the sensation of her hand on him. Then what she said registered and he came plummeting to earth. He jerked back. "What?"

"I need you to get some information on a license plate number."

"Ann, what are you talking about? Whose number and why do you need it?" He leaned back against the couch and glared at her.

"Well." She pouted for a moment, then slowly churned out the reason for her request.

Sterling jumped up. "No. Absolutely not." He started pacing and shaking his head. "I don't want to get involved in any of you women's eye-spy business."

Ann Marie got up and walked over to him. She pressed her tiny body against his. "Why can't you do me this one favor?" she purred. "Even though it's for my friend it may as well be for me. If I didn't think it was important I would never have asked. She deserves to know."

"Why doesn't she just ask him?" he said, his tone not as harsh.

"What if he lies?"

"What if he tells the truth? All men don't lie, Ann. All men are not Terrance."

She flinched, then lowered her eyes. "I know

that," she said softly. "You've proven that to me." She caressed his cheek. "I only want the same thing for my friend. I want her to finally have the same thing that I have—no doubts."

Sterling sighed heavily. "Fine. I'll make a few calls. But I'm warning you, Ann, sometimes you have to be careful what you wish for."

She reached up on tiptoe and kissed his lips. "I'll make it worth your while."

He fought down a grin. "You'd better. Come on in the bedroom, I have a trick I want to show you."

Chapter 14

Barbara yawned and stretched her arms high over her head. She'd been making calls all morning to reschedule appointments. More than half of the hospital rehab staff had called out for the day because of the weather. It was pure determination and the fact that she didn't want to sit home alone thinking about Wil that got her to her job at the hospital. It had taken her more than an hour maneuvering the mass transit system as there was no way she was going to drive.

She'd just made her last phone call when the sole assistant, who'd shown up because she lived in walking distance, stuck her head in the door.

"You have a visitor."

Barbara's eyes widened. "A visitor? You have got to be kidding. I thought I canceled all the appointments for today."

"He didn't have an appointment."

Barbara pushed up from her seat. "Who is it?"

"Mr. Townsend," she said, obviously impressed. Although famous athletes walking through New York University's rehab center was a commonplace occurrence, it still thrilled some to see them up close, especially for newcomers like today's assistant.

Barbara felt a rush of heat followed by alarm. She swallowed, trying to think of a way out of it. What was the point in running? She needed to put an end to this once and for all. She straightened her shoulders.

"Tell him to come in."

Moments later Michael walked in the door.

"Hello, Barbara." He closed the door behind him. "I know—another surprise visit."

"You seem to be making this a habit."

"I thought this would be neutral territory."

"Michael—"

"Wait, just hear me out." He crossed the room toward her and she backed up. He stopped. "Look, I know I made some mistakes when it came to me and you. I acted jealous and immature. But I can't stop thinking about you. I want the chance to work things out between us. I know it can work and I want you to let me prove it to you."

This can't be happening. "Michael, I can't go through this with you." She started gathering her belongings. "You shouldn't have come here." She took her coat off the hook.

He blocked her exit. "Just look at me. For one minute just look me in the eye and tell me that what we had didn't mean anything to you. Tell me that you don't still think about me, about us."

The words stuck in her throat. She wanted to spit them out but nothing happened.

"Let me at least drive you home."

"How do you know I didn't drive my own car?"

He grinned. "Because I know you don't like driving in bad weather, especially snow."

It was a little thing, something that you wouldn't ordinarily pay attention to. But it was always the little things that Michael remembered about her like the fact that she loved sleeping late on Sunday mornings and reading the paper in bed. Or that she really had an aversion to white wine because it gave her a headache or that as much as she loved flowers she had a brown thumb so he would replace the plants and flowers he bought for her on a regular basis. Yeah, the little things.

"Okay," she said finally. "Let me clock out."

They walked out together to his Navigator that was parked in the hospital lot. He helped her into the passenger seat, and for an instant it felt just like old times. *But it isn't,* Barbara reminded herself.

"The plows did a lot of cleaning up, but the side streets are still pretty bad," Michael said. He glanced at her.

"How did you even know I would be at work today?"

"Because I know how dedicated you are to your job and if there was any way you could get here you would. I was a patient of yours, remember?"

How well she remembered.

"How serious is it between you and Wil?"

Her muscles tightened. "Why?"

"I want to know what I'm up against. Is it serious?"

"It's really none of your concern, Michael."

"Everything about you and your life concerns me. I'm still very much in love with you."

She stared straight ahead.

"Do you love him?"

She didn't answer.

"Does he make you feel the way I made you feel?"

"Don't do this."

"You can't answer me because you don't want to tell me the truth. But the truth is in your eyes. It's in the way your body reacts when I touch you…like this." He let his finger stroke her cheek.

She grabbed his hand but didn't move it from her cheek. "Michael…don't."

"I know you like it when I touch you."

This time she pushed his hand away. "What do you want from me?" Her luminous eyes snapped in time to the sharpness of her voice.

"I want you to admit how you feel about me and come back to me. I know I can make you happy. I made you happy before. You can't deny that."

Her heart was racing so fast she thought she'd faint. "We've been down this road."

"Yeah, and we got off it much too soon. Listen, I'm in town for two days. Today and tomorrow. We leave for Philly tomorrow night. I have a game tonight at the Garden. I want to see you before I go."

"You're seeing me now."

"No. Come to my hotel tomorrow afternoon. I'll order room service for lunch. I just want to talk."

"Michael, I can't do that."

"You can if you want to. I'm staying at the Plaza. I'll be there all day tomorrow." He pulled up in front of her building on Morningside Drive.

The instant the car slowed, Barbara reached for the door handle.

Michael jumped out of the car and quickly came around to her side. He pulled her door open, lifted her up and over the snowbank at the curb. He held her against him for a moment too long before setting her on her feet.

Barbara could barely breathe. Her gaze slowly rose until it met and collided with his. Her thoughts short-circuited. Nothing made sense.

"If you don't come, then I'll know it's finally over and I swear to you I'll never bother you again."

"Goodbye, Michael." She turned but he grabbed her arm and shoved something in her hand.

"I promised Chauncey tickets the next time I was in town."

She looked at them as if they might burst into flames.

"I keep my promises."

She clasped the tickets in her hand and started toward the front door across the slippery pavement with as much style as she could summon.

"The Plaza," he called out. "Room 1608."

She dared not turn around. If she did she knew there was no turning back.

Chapter 15

Elizabeth was in her sparkling new kitchen preparing dinner for her and Ron. The spa was closed for the day because of the weather and Elizabeth was thrilled. Both she and Ron had been working so hard recently that even when they did spend time together, which was often, they were too tired to really enjoy each other. Although she was happy to spend a long overdue day with Barbara and she loved her friend dearly, it couldn't compare to spending time with her man.

She grinned to herself. *Her man.* Humph, when was the last time she was able to say that and hadn't meant her husband? She pulled open the door to the range and basted the chicken. It was almost done and the potatoes that hugged the sides of the roasting pan would be absolutely perfect.

In less than a year her flawless life had done a complete three-hundred-and-sixty-degree turn. Her marriage to her high school sweetheart had crumbled like a Ritz cracker. She'd had to sell the house that she'd lived in for nearly twenty years and made into a home, to figure out how she was going to support herself and live a life as a single woman.

After she'd gotten over the hurt, then came the show and then the realization that she didn't have the luxury of time to feel sorry for herself. She wasn't the first woman whose husband cheated on her and broke up a home, and she wouldn't be the last.

Her friends and opening the spa had been her lifeline, and finding Ron standing on the board-walk ready to pull her ashore was her salvation.

"Sure smells good up in here," Ron said, coming up behind her and nibbling her ear.

She giggled and swatted him away. "I thought you were unpacking the books."

"All done. Thought I'd let you decide where you wanted stuff."

"The chicken has about fifteen minutes. Let me take a quick peek." She scurried behind him into the living room.

Ron had been working on the built-in bookshelf for weeks. It stood from floor to ceiling with twelve rows of shelving. It gleamed in an identical match to her parquet flooring, making it appear as if it were an outgrowth of the floor itself. He'd even attached a ladder so that she could reach the uppermost shelf.

"It's finally dry. I just anchored in the last shelf. What do you think?"

She covered her mouth in awe. "It's…beautiful." She spun around and hugged him around his neck so tight he gasped for air.

"If I'm going to get that kind of thanks, I think I need to build more stuff around here."

"Anytime." Then she looked around at the stacks of books that practically covered the entire living room floor. "Wow, looks like I have my work cut out for me."

"You definitely have a lot of books." He bent down and picked up a copy of *Huckleberry Finn*. "How old is this?"

"My grandmother gave it to me when I was about eight."

"Hmm, pretty old," he teased.

She punched him in the arm. "Not funny."

He reached for another book. "Octavia Butler."

"Love her imagination. There will never be another writer like her. She was a pioneer in the sci-fi world, especially for black writers."

He actually started looking at the titles and topics. She had books on what appeared to be everthing: romance, mystery, poetry, short story collections, first editions. Books in Spanish and French. There were books on art, cooking, interior design, finance.

"Have you actually read all these?" he asked in amazement.

"Most of them."

"Impressive. I have a collection of *Sports Illustrated*." He chuckled.

"Matthew used to buy me books all the time. And every time we traveled I bought a book from that city or country." She squatted down and checked the spines of a few books and began putting them in groups according to subject or genre. "When I was in college I wasn't sure what I wanted to be. I had so many interests. So I bought books on whatever struck my fancy at the time. By the time I graduated my parents had to use the spare bedroom for my books." She laughed lightly at the memory.

"What about you? You never talk a lot about school and 'back home' other than your revolutionary days."

"Not much to tell. Came up poor. Stayed that way for most of my growing up years. Didn't finish college, had to work. Never been out of the country or any farther than California." He blew out a breath. "Not much of a privileged life."

She took a quick glance at him over her shoulder. "Privileged? Do you think I was privileged?"

He crossed the room. "Maybe not, just different." He looked out the window. "Seems like you had a pretty good life. All the pieces always fit."

"Looks are deceiving." She waited. "Ron...what are you not saying?" She slowly stood up.

"Do you ever wonder why he cheated?" he asked, totally detouring the conversation.

She flinched. "I used to, all the time. Couldn't come up with a solid answer, though."

"He was a fool."

"Water under the bridge."

"He and I are nothing alike."

She reached out and clasped his upper arm. "Look at me."

He turned his head toward her. "No, you aren't. And I don't want you to be."

"I'll never be able to give you the kind of life you've been used to, the kind of life you had with him and the girls."

"I don't want that kind of life anymore. I lived it and I'm done. Ron, what's wrong? What brought all this on?"

"Forget it." The corner of his mouth quirked upward. "Just a bout of male ego." He put his arm around her and hugged her close to his body, then kissed the top of her head. He sniffed the air. "I smell dinner. I'll have much more strength to help with these books after a good meal."

"Right this way."

While they were eating dinner, Elizabeth asked, "Why didn't you ever marry?"

"I almost did. Things didn't work out."

"What happened?"

"She wanted more than what I could give her." He looked into her eyes, then glanced away.

"And you think I'm going to do the same thing?" she asked gently.

He didn't respond.

"Ron. If there is one thing I know—that's who I am. I was never one who wanted things, a lot of money, cars, and all the frills. Sure, that's the kind of life I lived, but I found out the hard way it was all a facade. And my happiness, my fulfillment as a woman is more important than anything money and name recognition can buy."

"I'm a real simple man, Ellie. A hardworking simple man. I took a look at all those books, heard you talk about all the places you've been." He slowly shook his head. "And all of a sudden I was that guy again who just didn't quite cut it."

She got up from her seat and came around to his side and sat on his lap. "Listen, buddy, you make me happy. You make my heart and spirit sing. I get all giddy and excited when I know I'm going to see you or when you walk in the door. You *see* me." She cupped his chin. "Do you know how much that means to me? I'd forgotten how much I needed to be *seen* until I saw my reflection in your eyes."

He reached up and ran his fingers through her hair, pulling her toward him. His voice was thick with emotion. "I see you."

"I know." She touched her lips to his, and her heart leaped in her chest. Those words were pure music to her ears. She eased back with a gleam in her eyes and a seductive smile moving across her mouth. "Why don't you come with me? And let me know if you like what I have to show you." She took his hand and pulled him to his feet.

"Hmm, nothing like dessert after a good meal...."

They walked arm in arm to her bedroom. When they reached the door, Ron stopped. Elizabeth turned to him. "What's wrong?"

"There's been something I wanted to talk to you about, even though I swore I wouldn't say anything. But I think if I told you, you'd know the best way to handle it."

"What is it?"

"It's about Ali…."

Ann Marie was in her home office looking over some real estate listings for Ali when Sterling came in the room. He stood in the doorway.

She swiveled the chair around. "Hey, handsome."

He stepped inside. "I only did this for you." He handed her a piece of paper folded in half. "Like I said, sometimes when you go looking for trouble you find more than you bargained for. I hope it's worth it." He walked out.

Ann Marie took the paper, unfolded it, and looked at Sterling's neat handwriting. Her heart sank. For a moment she really thought about putting it in the shredder and telling Stephanie that Sterling couldn't find out anything. But she would know. Maybe Tony was right. When you looked for trouble you were bound to find it.

Chapter 16

Stephanie was curled up on her couch watching a rerun of the movie *Heat* with Al Pacino and Robert DeNiro, two of her favorite actors. They were just up to the chase scene on the airfield when her phone rang. She bit down on a cookie, the last one that she'd found in the package in the back of the cabinet, before reaching for the phone.

She looked at the caller ID before answering. "Hey, Ann Marie." She chewed her cookie wishing that it could have lasted a while longer.

Her stomach growled in protest. "What's up? You finally let that poor man out of bed?"

"I, um, Sterling got the information."

Stephanie slowly sat up straight. She pointed the remote at the television and muted the volume. "Well..."

"The car belongs to Leslie Dixon."

Stephanie felt the air swoosh out of her lungs.

"She lives in New Haven, Connecticut."

"Leslie." She let the name roll over her tongue. She knew who she was, now what?

"Steph, are you all right?"

"He's married...with a child," she said, her voice detached.

"It doesn't mean he's married. It could be a relative, a sister, a cousin."

"Then why didn't he ever tell me about her? He's never mentioned a sister."

"I'm sure there's a reason, Steph. Don't jump to conclusions. You need to talk to him, tell him what you know and let him explain."

"What am I going to say, Ann," she yelled, "that I had friend run the license plate number of a car I saw you get in because I didn't trust you to tell me the truth? God!" She shook her head wildly. "I should never have let you talk me into this."

Ann Marie was beginning to feel the same way. "Stephanie, I'm sorry. But it may not be what we think at all and you'll never know if you don't talk to him."

"I gotta go." She hung up the phone before Ann Marie could say anything else. "Leslie Dixon." Heat scorched her throat and stung her eyes.

She thought back to when they'd first met. She'd always believed that all that instant attraction mumbo jumbo was ridiculous, but that was what happened to her when she met Tony. Something inside her clicked. She'd just extricated herself from her torrid relationship with Conrad, and Tony was like an oasis in the desert. Until she noticed his wedding ring.

All her warning alarms went off and she'd vowed to herself that after Conrad she'd never get involved with a married man again. And she didn't. She kept things strictly business between them even though Tony tried on several occasions to take things to the next step.

But then on the night of the grand opening of

Pause for Men he'd told her that his wife had died five years earlier and until he'd met her, there'd never been a reason to take it off.

She'd believed him. She'd wanted to believe him. But now she didn't know what to believe. What she was sure of was that she couldn't sit in the house a moment longer.

She marched off to her bedroom, put on a pair of jeans and a heavy sweater, then went and got her coat and purse and headed out.

She wandered down Amsterdam Avenue, sidestepping puddles and piles of snow. It was already beginning to melt. In a few days the city would be a complete slushy mess. There was a new Thai restaurant on 120th Street. She had passed the point of starving hours earlier, but maybe some food would do her good.

As was typical of intrepid New Yorkers, the stores and restaurants were open, all doing what appeared to be a brisk business. The Thai restaurant was no exception. There was actually a line at the takeout counter. She was finally able to place her order and waited nearly a half hour before it was ready. By then she'd lost what little appetite she'd had.

With her bag in hand she made her way slowly back home. She reached the front door of her building and was hunting around in her purse for her keys. Just as she was putting the key in the lock she felt someone come up behind her.

She whirled around and came face-to-face with Conrad. She yelped in alarm.

He held up his palms. "I'm sorry, I didn't mean to scare you. I was sitting out in my car debating whether or not I should ring the bell when I saw you walk up."

"I have a restraining order against you. If you don't get the hell away from me, I'm calling the police." She went for her cell phone and instantly realized she'd left it in the house next to her bed. "Leave, Conrad. Now!"

"She left me, Steph."

Stephanie frowned in confusion. "What are you talking about?"

"Marilyn, she left me and she took the kids. I didn't know what to do. Where to go. You're the only one I could talk to."

She'd never seen him like this: broken, contrite, and vulnerable.

"I never thought...I don't know what I thought," he mumbled.

She could tell he'd been crying, actually crying. The rims of his eyes were red and the five o'clock shadow was now a full day's growth. This wasn't the Conrad Hendricks that she knew. The man she knew was strong, aggressive, arrogant to the point of being abusive.

"I just want to talk. Can I come up for a few minutes? I swear I won't touch you."

With the frame of mind she was in, all twisted and distorted, a few minutes would turn into a few hours. She had to remind herself that as hurt as he might appear, this was the same man who'd held her down on her living room floor and had sex with her even though she'd said no.

"Stephanie, please?"

She blinked and he came back into focus. "No, Conrad. You can't come up. I'm sorry. I'm sorry about everything. Us, your wife, your kids. We're both responsible for where we are today and we have to deal with the consequences of our actions." She sighed with resignation. "What more is there to say than that?" She almost reached out and touched him, but she wouldn't dare. "You'll get through it." She turned, opened the door, and closed it gently but firmly behind her.

When she got up to her apartment, she put down her bag, went straight to the phone, and dialed Tony's number. The phone rang three times before he picked up. She heard traffic noises in the background.

"We need to talk," was all she'd said.

"I know. I'm about an hour and a half away. Can I come over when I get into the city?"

"I'll be waiting."

Chauncey was totally absorbed in the game. He was keeping his eyes on the players waiting for Michael to make his entry onto the court.

"There he is!" he shouted out to his dad, pointing to the television.

Wil pretended to be engrossed in a magazine that truly held no interest for him, but he couldn't help stealing surreptitious glances at the screen and compare himself to Michael Townsend in every way.

He could see why Barbara was attracted to him. What woman wouldn't be? He was young, fit, handsome, famous, and wealthy. All the things that he wasn't.

"Oh man, did you see that move Michael put on Maubury!" He slapped his palm against his forehead. "Nasty! Shook that brotha right out of his Nikes." He fell back against the couch and cracked up laughing.

Wil couldn't stand it another minute. He got up and went into the kitchen. He walked around the table several times as if he were playing musical chairs until he finally decided to get a beer. He took out an icy cold Corona and twisted off the cap. He tossed it toward the open garbage can. The top bounced around the rim and popped out.

Wil shook his head in disgust. "Figures."

Just as he was about to take a swallow he glanced down at his belly that was certainly not what it once was. He clenched his teeth.

Maybe that's what Barbara needed, a young buck. Men did it all the time when they reached his age. Besides, what could he do for Barbara on a mailman's salary? In five more years, he'd be ready to retire and live off his pension. Michael could wrap her in furs. All he could offer was wool.

He looked at the bottle in his hands, brought it to his lips, and chugged it down.

Barbara was channel surfing when she landed on the game in progress. A pang of guilt stabbed at her for holding on to the tickets and not giving them to Chauncey. But if she did she'd have to say how she got them—that she'd seen Michael—explain it all. She shouldn't have to explain anything. She was grown.

Then why didn't she call Wil and tell him about the tickets? For the same reason that she was going to see Michael at the Plaza the following day—she didn't want Wil to know.

Chapter 17

It was almost one in the morning by the time Tony got back to New York. The two-hour drive had turned into a grueling four. He should have taken the train like he started to instead of being Mr. Macho and renting a car for the drive back. He was exhausted but he had no intention of going home until he talked to Stephanie.

He circled the block four times before he found a space that he could squeeze into. The snowdrifts made a difficult job that much harder.

He grabbed his overnight bag from the backseat, locked up the car, and set the alarm.

He'd been rehearsing what he'd planned to say to Stephanie for the entire ride. But every version that went through his head sounded so weak and selfish. But that's what he'd been these past five years—weak and selfish—though those days were behind him. He only hoped that it wasn't too late for him and Stephanie. Her request to talk sounded like more of an ultimatum than an invitation.

Tony trudged across the street to her building, pushed through the first door, and pressed her bell. He hoped she was still awake. Stephanie was extra miserable when she was awakened out of a good sleep. He'd barely lifted his finger from the bell before he was buzzed in.

Moments later he stood in front of her apartment door. He started to knock just as the door was pulled open.

"Hi," he said, totally unsure of what kind of reception he was going to get.

"I didn't think you were coming." She stepped aside to let him in.

He walked in. "I said I would."

"You've said a lot of things." She shut the door. It sounded like a cannon to Tony.

He took off his coat and draped it over his arm, unsure of how long he would be staying.

"You can hang up your coat. This is going to take a while." She walked past him and into the living room. She sat on the love seat and waited.

Tony came into the room with his hands in his pockets. "You want to start or should I?"

"Why did you lie to me?" she fired at him, her eyes blazing and her heart racing a mile a minute.

"Lie to you, about what?"

"About your life, your real life."

Did she know? How could she?

"I came to your apartment. I saw you and *her*."

For a minute it didn't register. "I don't know what you're talking about."

"Is that who you're with when you say you're with a client...your wife?"

He felt as if he'd been kicked. "My wife?" He shook his head in confusion and denial. "My wife...Kim died five years ago. I told you that." He stepped closer.

"Are you sure her name isn't Leslie?"

"Leslie? Oh man...Leslie isn't my wife, Steph, she's my sister."

For an instant the wind rushed out of her sail. "Right, why should I believe you?" she asked with much less bite, suddenly doubting everything she'd seen, heard, and done in the past twenty-four hours.

"Because I'm telling you the truth." He came over to her and stooped down to eye level. "Leslie is my sister. And if you saw what I think you saw, the little girl is my daughter—Joy."

Her mouth opened but nothing came out. *Daughter*. "I don't understand," she finally stammered. "You never said you had a daughter. Where does she live? Why isn't she with you?"

"That's what I want to talk to you about." Slowly he stood up and walked to the opposite side of the coffee table and sat down on the couch. He leaned forward and braced his arms on his thighs. "I never told you much about Kim because it hurt too much," he began. Hesitantly and with great pain, he told Stephanie how they'd met and fallen in love. He told her all about Kim's illness and her mother's vehement refusal to accept him in her daughter's life.

He told her about Kim's miscarriages and the final pregnancy that cost her life.

Stephanie fought back tears as she listened and felt every bit of the agony and remorse that she heard in his voice.

"I know it's a selfish thing to admit, but every time I looked at my daughter I saw Kim. I blamed myself for her death, and as much as I love my daughter a part of me blamed her too. I knew she needed love and a solid home, and I knew that I was in no emotional shape to give them to her. My sister said she would take her and raise her until I was ready."

"You could have told me. I would have understood. I could have helped you."

He shook his head. "So many times I wanted to, but when I saw how devoted you were to Samantha even with all that she's dealing with, and for me to admit to you that I couldn't take care of my own daughter…I didn't want to see the look in your eyes. You deal with the guilt you feel about your sister even though it's cost you so much personally, financially, and emotionally. How could I face you and not be willing to do the same thing?"

"I grew up without my father. And it has affected me in ways that I may never fully understand. I know it has a lot to do with how I feel about commitment and men in general—you can't stick with them because they're not to be trusted. And if you put your heart and your love into their hands they will walk away. Just like my father did. Just like you did to your daughter." Her eyes accused, tried and convicted him. "So why now? Why tell me now?"

"My time for running is over. I don't want to do it anymore. I can't. I want to be the father that my daughter needs and deserves on a full-time basis. And I want to be the man that you need and deserve. That can't happen if there are secrets between us. It's time that I forgave myself so that I can live—completely."

Stephanie got up. "I don't know what to think right now or how to feel. I need time."

He nodded. "I understand." He got up to leave.

"You don't have to go. It's late and I know you're exhausted." She waited a beat. "You can sleep on the couch. I don't think I'm ready to sleep with you yet."

His face went through a series of expressions and finally settled on acceptance. "Sure."

"You know where the blankets and sheets are." She turned and headed to her bedroom before she changed her mind and invited him to come with her.

"Steph?"

She stopped.

"Why did you come to my apartment? You never told me."

Stephanie lifted her chin a notch. "I came to tell you that I'm scared as all hell and that I love you."

She was gone so fast Tony wasn't sure if he'd imagined what he'd just heard. He just stood there. Frozen in place. *I love you.* He'd said the words to her dozens of times, but she'd never until that moment said them to him.

He flopped back down on the couch. Maybe there was hope for them. They could work through it.

Stephanie sat on the side of her bed gripping the mattress for dear life. She'd said it. She'd said out loud what she'd only thought to herself. She was shaking all over. A giddy sensation of euphoria flowed through her. She'd never said that to any man in her life. Never. The feeling was so new and uncharted she didn't know how to manage it.

She pressed her fist to her mouth to keep from screaming. She was in love. It was official. She glanced toward her bedroom door. That still didn't excuse Tony for lying to her all these months. Well, maybe not out-and-out lying but hiding the truth, which was just as bad.

It pained her deeply to imagine a little girl growing up without her dad. What did she look like? she wondered. Was she smart? Was she big or small for her age? Would his daughter accept her? Was she creative like her father?

Suddenly she jumped up from the bed and marched out front. Tony jerked to attention.

"What if she doesn't like me?"

A smile burst across his face. He got up and walked over to her. He ran his eyes over her face, seeing real concern in her expression but also a hopefulness.

"She'll love you," he said softly. "Just like I do."

Stephanie pressed her head against his chest

and closed her eyes. His arms wrapped around her and pulled her so close they could feel each other's heartbeat pounding in rhythm with each other.

His hands caressed her back, her waist, her hips in gentle up-and-down motions. He leaned back and looked down into her eyes. "If you let me, I'll prove it to you every day for the rest of our lives."

"I like the sound of that," she whispered.

He lowered his head and took her mouth in a kiss filled with all the love and desire he had in his heart. She moved against him and linked her arms up and around his neck. His tongue moved in slow motion with hers.

Reluctantly she pulled back and looked up at him. "If we're going to make this work, if I'm going to be your woman and you're my man, there can't be any more secrets between us. Ever."

"Promise."

"In that case we have some making up to do."

"I'd like nothing more." He kissed her long and deep without restraint. She moaned against his mouth, tugged his shirt out from his pants, and ran her hands up along his chest and around his back. He grabbed the hem of her sweater and pulled it up and over her head, then tossed it to the floor. She didn't have on a bra and his senses went into overdrive. She fumbled with the buckle on his belt until she loosened it, then pulled it through the loops and tossed it on top of her discarded sweater.

Tony pulled down his zipper and then hers. She wiggled out of her pants until they pooled at her ankles.

"I want you," he groaned against her pliant mouth.

"Show me," she commanded.

He hooked his thumbs beneath the elastic band of her panties and inched them down over her hips.

"Touch me," she whispered.

His fingers gently caressed her folds, parted the tender lips, and slid up into the wet well that throbbed for his touch.

She trembled and pressed her pelvis against his hand, rotating her hips, needing more of what he was giving her. She widened her thighs and he probed deeper.

Heat engulfed her. She reached for him and sighed deep in her throat when she felt how hard and ready he was. She couldn't wait. She pulled him with her down to the floor and rolled him over onto his back. She positioned herself above him, then eased down, inch by maddening inch, until she was filled.

"Ooooh," he hollered. "Yessss."

She rode him slow and steady, needing to feel every pulse and beat.

He grabbed her hips and pushed her solidly down on his erection, refusing to let her simply have her way with him. He held her in place as he moved up and in her in hot circles.

She reared back, her body bending nearly in half, her lush breasts pointing to the heavens. "Ohhh, baaaby…all of you, all of you."

Tony let her hips go and reached out for those delicious fruits that seemed to be calling his name. He tweaked her nipples between his thumbs and forefingers and her entire body vibrated. The muscles in her neck popped up like ropes beneath her skin. Her mouth opened but no sound escaped, the ecstasy so intensely beautiful it defied sound.

If I Were Your Woman

Witnessing the splendor of her climax set off his own, and the explosive release washed away all their doubts and fears and bound them together in a love that they readily admitted.

At some point they gathered enough energy to get up off the floor to crawl under the mounds of fluffy covers.

Her body was half wrapped around his, her head pressed against his heart.

He stroked her hair as he relived their incredible lovemaking session. It just seemed to get better and more intense each time. And he didn't think it was possible.

"Thank you," she said.

"For what?"

"For being patient and not giving up on us…and thank you for telling me about your daughter…and Kim. I know it wasn't easy."

"But you listened. That's what's important."

She sighed, contented.

"You know I wanted to ask you… How did you find out about Leslie?"

She looked up at him and grinned. "A girl's gotta have at least one secret."

Chapter 18

Barbara had been watching the clock all morning in between tending her heavy caseload of rehab patients. She'd slept in fits and starts during the night, debating the veracity of what she'd planned to do. More times than she could count she'd internally voted against going to the Plaza, but the practical side of her understood that going to see Michael was no longer an option but a necessity.

She'd arranged her therapy schedule to allow her an extra half hour for lunch and hoped that would give her the time she needed. She finished up with her last patient for the morning.

"I have a few errands to run on my lunch break," she said to her assistant. "So I'm going to be taking a little extra time. But I don't have another patient until three."

"No problem. I brought my lunch with me so I'll hold down the office in case anything comes up."

"Thanks. See you in a few."

Barbara hurried out to the parking lot and located her car. While she waited for it to warm up she went over what she planned to say and all the possible scenarios that could arise.

She drew in a breath of resolve, put the car in gear, and slowly pulled out. Getting from the East Side of Manhattan to the West Side was nerve-racking at best. Although the snow had begun to melt, the roads were still a challenge and the traffic was slow. What would have been a twenty-minute ride turned into forty. And Barbara's nerves were frazzled.

Finally she spotted the grand hotel up ahead and had to traverse the circular approach to the Plaza. She pulled up in front and was truly appreciative of the luxuries of the wealthy. A valet came up to her car, took her keys, and promised to take good care of her vehicle.

Barbara walked into the massive lobby of the Plaza that had been the backdrop for many movies with its ornate decoration and almost regal staff.

She tried to look inconspicuous as she searched for the bank of elevators. The last thing she wanted was for anyone to know that she was going up to see Michael or ask to help her in some way. She found the right set of elevators and stepped on, keeping her eyes on the floor when other hotel guests stepped on.

Finally the elevator arrived on the sixteenth floor. She checked the directional signs on the wall and turned left down the hushed corridor.

There, 1608. She stood in front of the door. She looked left, then right, inhaled deeply, then knocked on the door. The door was opened almost immediately.

Michael took up the doorway. When she saw the light sparking in his eyes and the welcoming smile widening the mouth that she knew so well, she knew in an instant that coming here was the right thing to do.

"Come in. You look beautiful as always."

Her cheeks heated. She walked past him and into his suite.

The suite was something right off a late-night soap. White was the centerpiece color from the thick wool carpet to the silk drapes that adorned floor-to-ceiling windows to the sectional couch that could easily seat ten with room to spare. A white-lacquered bar took up one side of the room, but it was the black marble fireplace set against the winter white walls that was the focal point. A roaring fire blazed behind the grate.

"Can I get you something to drink?"

"Water would be fine," she said, her throat suddenly dry. She walked over to the couch and sat down stiffly on its edge, holding her purse in a death grip in her lap as if she expected it to be ripped from her hands. She looked around knowing. This was how he lived every day. Expensive hotels, all his needs met, travel, money, a home in Miami, and one he was having built on the island of Antigua. She could have it all, too. Any worries that she might have had about her financial future in her later years would be non-existent.

Michael strolled over to her and extended the crystal glass. "I won't bite. You can relax."

She glanced up and forced a smile. She took the glass. "Thank you," she murmured.

Michael started to sit next to her but changed his mind and moved farther away. He didn't want to crowd her and he wanted to be able to look into her eyes while they talked.

"How long can you stay?" he began.

She cleared her throat. "Not long. I have to get back to work."

"Oh." His tone reflected his disappointment. "I was hoping that we could spend the afternoon together. But I'm just happy you're here." He clasped his large hands together and leaned forward slightly. "These months that we've been apart have been harder on me than I imagined." He chuckled lightly. "Contrary to popular opinion, us jocks have feelings too." He stole a glance at her. "But the time apart also gave me time to think, think about why it didn't work—for you." He paused to gather his thoughts. "I realize now that I was on a full-court press from the beginning. You were the winning basket and I was going to make it no matter

what. And I was going to get past all your best
defenses. I don't think I ever gave you a chance
to show me your skills on the court." He ducked
his head for a moment. "Sorry for all the NBA
lingo, but I hope you understand what I'm trying
to tell you.

"I'm willing to back up, give you some space
so that you can be you. If you want to work,
work. If you don't want to move from New
York?" He shrugged. "No problem. What I'm
saying is I'm willing to compromise. I'm willing
to listen to the coach." He ran his tongue across
his lips.

If only they would have had this conversation
months ago, if only... "Mike...I can't begin to
tell you how much you have meant and mean
to me. You changed my life in so many ways.
I'd been sleepwalking for years content to be
alone except for my friends, and then you burst
into my life and I came face-to-face with the
sun." She studied her clenched hands. "I love
you and so many things about you. I've been in
lust with you." She smiled shyly, then looked
directly at him. "But I'm not *in* love with you."
She watched his hopeful expression fall and felt

her heart breaking. If she never knew before the depths of his feelings for her she understood them now. "I never was. I was captivated, mesmerized, swept away by the very notion of you and you wanting me. But that's not enough to build a relationship on." She swallowed over the knot building in her throat. She opened her purse and took out the velvet box. She set it down on the table. "I should have given this back to you a long time ago. It's a beautiful token of who we *were* to each other. But we both have to move on, and holding on to tokens of the past won't let us do that."

He smile was sad. "That's why I'll always love you and you'll always have a place in my heart because you never held back. You've been trying to tell me this for a long time. I wasn't listening." He stood. "But I am now." He reached out his hand.

Barbara stood up and took his hand. He gently pulled her toward him and held her tenderly against his chest. "He's a lucky man. And I'm man enough to step aside for good. All I want is for you to be happy."

She glanced up at him. "I am."

He nodded and kissed her forehead, then let her go. "Can I call you a car service?"

"No, I drove."

His eyes widened in surprise. "You drove?"

"Yeah, I'm working on confronting the things that challenge me."

He walked her to the door. "Listen, I'm a man of my word. I'll make sure that Chauncey gets season tickets to the Garden." He held up his hand when it looked as though she was going to object. I'll mail them."

She smiled. "Thanks."

He opened the door. "Maybe you'll even come one of these days. It would be great to look out and see you in the stands."

She pressed her finger to his chest. "I just might." She drew in a breath. "Goodbye, Michael."

"Goodbye."

She turned and slowly walked down the hallway, then picked up her pace. With each step her spirit grew lighter, her heart and conscience clearer. She pressed the bell for the elevator. She and Michael had done the goodbyes before they'd said all the words. But because she had not been totally clear in her heart and mind, she'd inadvertently left the door ajar. The elevator bell tinged. She stepped on. The door closed— finally.

Elizabeth sat behind the check-in desk going over the supply list. But her mind wasn't on what she was doing.

She and Ron had talked long into the night. He told her all about Ali and his connection to Stephanie. Ron told her that he was at a crossroads as to what to do. Ali had asked him not to say anything. He didn't feel it was right to keep something that important away from Stephanie, but didn't know the best way to approach her.

"I know I broke a promise," he'd said as they lay in bed together. "But there's no one else I would entrust this to. I value your judgment."

Elizabeth thought about that now. He and Matt were like night and day. She couldn't remember a time in their twenty-plus-year marriage that Matt had ever "valued her judgment" about anything more serious than the grocery list. She smiled to herself. So this is what it really felt like to be loved and valued.

She checked the time on the computer. Steph-

anie had called earlier and said that she would
come in at three and take over the front. It was
almost that now.

Elizabeth busied herself with filing and
counting the minutes. A little after three, Stephanie breezed in looking absolutely fabulous. She
was always stylish in her appearance, but today
without a doubt she looked like she was ready for
a photo shoot.

Her champagne-colored hair was feathered
around her face with the top in that spiked look
but classy. Her honey-toned skin was flawlessly
made up. She wore thigh-high black leather
boots over black leggings. And from beneath her
waist-length fox jacket bloomed a winter white
chenille sweater with a collar that rose almost up
to her cheeks. Every male she passed turned his
head in her direction.

"Well, where are you going or coming from?"
Elizabeth asked, looking her over in admiration.

She dramatically swept off her dark glasses,
then cracked up laughing. "Like that move, huh?
I've always wanted to do that."

"You're in a good mood. Something happen?"

"Yes, I'm in love! Can you believe it? Me,

Stephanie Moore, party girl, can't-tie-me-down extraordinaire."

"Whoa, and when did you get this revelation?"

"Last night. Maybe even before then but I just wasn't willing to admit it, not even to myself."

"Anyone I know?" Elizabeth teased.

Stephanie leaned on the counter. "As a matter of fact, he's good-looking, built, talented, fun, sexy—"

"Hey, watch it. That sounds like my man," she said with an exaggerated roll and pop of her neck.

Stephanie high-fived her. "I hear that."

"For real, though, girl, I'm happy for you. You deserve it. You've been through it, and Tony is a damned good guy. At least from where I'm standing."

"Yes, he is. So…everything cool around here? You ready to go on your break? I can actually stay the rest of the evening if you have things to do."

Stephanie was in such a good mood. Elizabeth didn't want to be the one to break her bubble, but she honestly believed that holding on to what she knew only delayed the inevitable. And she also knew how much Stephanie needed answers.

"Actually, I was going to let one of the part-timers cover the front. I wanted to talk to you about something."

"Oh." Her exuberant expression dwindled by degrees. "Is something wrong? Your whole aura changed."

"No, nothing like that but I have some news that I want to share with you. Let's go downstairs."

When they got to the office, Elizabeth closed the door. Stephanie spun around to face her. "What the hell is it? You're scaring me."

"Just sit down for a minute, okay?"

Reluctantly, Stephanie sat down. "Well?"

"We all know how you feel about growing up without your father and not knowing why he left…."

Stephanie's eyes widened.

"Ron's friend Ali…knows all about it. He doesn't know how to tell you. But I think you need to talk to him."

"What are you saying?"

"I'm saying Ali has the answers you've been looking for."

Ali, the man who'd rescued her, the one she'd met at the restaurant, the one who seemed so oddly familiar? She didn't know what to think. What could he know?

Stephanie finally focused on Elizabeth. "Um, Ron didn't tell you anything else?"

"No." She knew she was lying to her friend. Ron told her everything. But she wanted Stephanie to hear it all firsthand from Ali.

"I don't even know how to get in touch with him. I—" Her mind was so jumbled that she'd almost forgotten that she had his number. "I'm going to call him," she said, her voice suddenly paper thin. She kept nodding to herself as she fumbled around in her bag for her Axim as if to reconfirm what she was doing and if it was the right thing.

After several false starts she located it, turned it on, and scrolled for his number. She glanced up at Elizabeth who gave her a smile of encouragement and eased out the door.

Stephanie stared at the number for a few moments, thinking, debating with herself. Was Ali her father? Was that the reason he seemed so familiar to her? When she was growing up, her mother never kept pictures of her father and she only had a vague image of him when she was three or four years old. The only other person who would even have an inkling of what he looked like would be Samantha. There were no aunts or uncles, no grandmas or grandpas. For the most part she and Sam were orphans, having had to look out for themselves since their early teens when their mother simply stopped coming home.

She swallowed down the past, looked at the number, and punched it into her cell phone. Whatever he had to tell her would be more than she'd ever known. That much she was sure of.

"Hello?"

She froze. There was a lot of noise in the background, banging and yelling.

"Hello?"

"Um, this is Stephanie."

"How are you? I can barely hear you. I'm on a construction site."

"I understand. I was hoping we could talk… about my dad."

Chapter 19

Barbara finished up for the day at the hospital and prepared to go home. Her parting conversation earlier with Michael still rested with her. She had to admit it was certainly ego boosting to have a young man in love with you, especially at her age. But she knew deep in her heart that she needed more and needed to give more and that would never happen with Michael.

She had her evening all planned. Hopefully it wasn't too late to work things out with Wil, and if it was she would simply deal with it.

By the time she reached her apartment is was a bit after six. She had two hours to take her shower, get dressed, and make it on time.

She took her time with her bath and then soothed her frazzled nerves with aromatherapy body lotion. She painstakingly applied her makeup and was once again delighted that she'd cut her hair into such a manageable, not to mention sexy, do. She'd chosen her outfit with care. She didn't want to be too out there, but she still wanted to be noticed.

She checked the bedside clock. She had forty-five minutes to get there. But she wasn't going to chance her driving, so she called a taxi service. Her heart was in her throat for the entire trip and she silently prayed that her little plan didn't backfire.

Barbara arrived with time to spare. She was shown to her reserved table and waited. Every few minutes she checked her watch and was about ready to bust from the three glasses of water and the basket of bread she'd consumed.

She'd been there for more than a half hour and was beginning to think she should just leave, especially if the waitress came back one more time and asked what she'd like to order.

Despondent, she picked up her purse and had collected her coat from the back of her chair when she glimpsed movement coming in her direction. Her heart stood still when their gazes connected. *Please don't let him walk out.*

Wil stopped short when he spotted her and turned over his shoulder to scowl at his son, who was beaming with delight. He pushed his father forward until they stood in front of Barbara.

"Hi, Ms. Barbara, sorry we're late. Trying to get Dad out of the house on a weeknight is murder."

"Thank you," she whispered.

"What's this all about?" Wil grumbled.

"Why don't you sit down, Dad, and find out? Look, I gotta go. I have homework. Enjoy yourselves."

Wil looked totally flustered. He turned to Barbara. "You two set me up."

"Something like that," Barbara said. "Please sit down."

Wil huffed but finally sat. He folded his arms on the table. "Why am I here?"

She looked him right in the eyes. "So that I can tell you that the only man I want in my life is you. Nothing and no one can come between that. Not all the money, the fancy cars, hotels, trips…none of that. What makes me happy is you. I waited the better part of my adult life to find happiness. I lost you once. I don't plan to do it again."

Wil twisted his lips. "You look real good," he offered.

She grinned. "Is that right?"

"Pretty thing like you needs a real man to take care of her, love her, make her feel that she's the most important thing in his life and that if he lost her, he'd lose a part of his soul."

Barbara's eyes filled and before she could stop them, tears spilled over her lashes.

"I hope those are tears of happiness," he said, reaching across the table for her hand. "Because the last thing I ever want to do is cause you pain."

"They are," she said through her choked sob. "The happiest tears I've ever shed."

"Are you two ready to order now?"

Wil looked up at the young girl, then across at Barbara. "No, we're going to go home."

* * *

She should have called Tony so that he could be there with her. This was definitely not the greatest part of town. She paced in front of the building to both keep warm and keep her mind from running in a million directions at once. He said he'd meet her here by eight o'clock. It was almost that now. She hugged her arms to her body and stomped her feet.

A yellow cab pulled up. Moments later Ali stepped out.

"Hope you weren't waiting too long. You know how hard it is for a black man to get a cab in New York."

"No problem," she said, her nerves jumping up and down.

"Let's get you out of this cold." He trotted up the stairs and pushed open the rickety front door that had no lock, nor the second door. "It's not much but it's warm. Once you see it, you'll know why I want to get a place soon. I hope you're in good shape. The elevator is out and I'm on the fifth floor."

Stephanie was too nervous to respond, she just followed him up the musty-smelling stairs.

Finally they reached his door. She looked around. The hallway was a color that she couldn't quite make out. It might have been green at one point. She heard yelling coming from one end of the hallway and inhaled the smell of food cooked over years that had seeped into every crevice of the building.

He stuck his key in the lock, jiggled it a few times before it would give way, then opened the door and switched on the light.

Stephanie walked in cautiously behind him. It was better than she'd envisioned. It was clean and she could tell that he tried his best to spruce the room up with a few plants and a bright bed-spread on the single bed.

He hurried across the room and pulled out a folding chair that was stacked against the wall. He opened it for her, then took one for himself.

"Make yourself as comfortable as possible. Can I fix you some tea to take the chill off?"

She shook her head. "No, thank you."

He slowly sat down opposite her. "To be truthful I never thought I'd see you again. Last time I saw you and your sister ya'll were about four years old."

"What do you mean?" Her heart thudded wildly. "Saw us where?"

"With your mama and your daddy. I was your dad's best friend. We grew up together in Atlanta. Franklin and Melvin, thick as thieves."

"You knew my father?"

"Sure did."

"Where is he, what happened to him?"

"Your mother and father married right out of high school. Your dad loved your mother like nobody's business. And before you knew it, your mama popped out not one but two beautiful twin girls." He smiled at the memory and shook his head. "Your father was so proud and his chest was sticking out so far he could barely button his shirts."

"What was he like?"

Ali leaned back on the metal chair. "Your dad was a damned good musician. He could play the piano in a way that would make you think you'd gone to heaven. He used to play in some of the clubs around town to make extra money on the weekends."

"He played piano?" she asked in awe.

"Yep, and could outrun anyone on the entire

track team in high school. He was a good man, a hardworking man that would have done anything for his wife and kids."

Her throat muscles constricted. "Then why did he leave us?"

"He didn't leave, not the way you think or what your mother may have told you. He got drafted for the war in Vietnam. When he left it nearly killed your mother. She was as fragile as anything and relied on Franklin for every breath she took. When he went off to war a piece of her mind went with him."

Stephanie's gaze raced around the room trying to find somewhere to land. Her father went to war. Her mother went crazy. It was all too much. But she had to know more. She wanted to know it all. She deserved to know after all these years.

"I tried to do the best I could for her and you girls. I'd bring food, clean the house, take care of you and your sister when your mother would get into one of her spells."

"Spells?"

"Sometimes she would just sit by the window for days, not eat, not wash, not even take care of her kids. She'd just stare out the window looking for Franklin."

Stephanie jumped and began to pace. "My mother was crazy."

"Your mother's heart was so broken there was no way to fix it."

"Then one day I came by the house and everyone was gone. Nothing there but the curtains sailing in the breeze. I wrote to your father and he flipped. His platoon sergeant said he ran into an open field and stepped on a land mine."

She gasped in horror.

"When he finally came home—"

"Came home! My father came home?"

Ali nodded his head. "Lost his leg, but he came home. But that war had done things to him. He saw things that no one should have to see in this lifetime. And it changed him. When he came home to nothing and the only thing to occupy his thoughts was the horrors that he'd seen, he shut himself off from the world."

She let the question hang on her lips, wanting to ask it but afraid of the answer. "Is my father still alive."

Ali paused for a long moment. "Yes. I lost track of him for years but he's in the V.A. hospital in Austin, Texas."

She covered her mouth with her hands. "Oh my God, oh my God," she cried. Her body shook as the sobs overtook her. All these years, all these years… She wept like a baby, and Ali held her in his arms just like he did when she was a little girl and the feeling in Stephanie's heart was oh so familiar.

"Are you going to be all right? I can drive you home and take the train or bus back over here," Ali said.

"No, I'll be fine. I need some time alone to process it all."

He nodded in understanding. "If there's anything that I can do you just let me know."

She stared into his eyes. "It's been so long. How did you even know it was me?"

"You look just like your daddy," he said gently. "He was my best friend in the world. I'd never forget his face. The first time I caught a glimpse of you coming out of the spa I had to do a double take. I followed you that day that you almost fell in the snow. I had to see you up close.

Then when I saw you at the restaurant I knew for sure. You hold your head to the side like your mother did every time she was thinking about something. Ron told me about Sam. I'm so sorry."

"Maybe you can go with me to see her some-times."

"I'd like that."

"I'd better go." She reached up and kissed his cheek. Thank you, Uncle M." She stepped back and looked into his eyes. She'd swear he was going to cry.

"You remembered?" he said, his voice thick with emotion.

"Yes, I did."

The first thing she did the minute she walked into her apartment was call Tony.

"Babe, I have so much to tell you."

"What's going on? You sound like you've been crying."

"I have but it's all good."

"I don't understand. What happened?"

"Just get your fine self over here and I'll tell you all about it."

"Don't have to ask me twice."

"I will tell you this."

"What."

"I do belong to somebody, Tony." Her voice cracked into tiny pieces. "They did love me. They did."

Chapter 20

Friday night two weeks later

It was girls' night and par for the course the fabulous foursome were gathered at Barbara's house. Terri had been called out of town on business, so she couldn't join in the festivities, but promised to be there next time.

The music was popping, food was in abundance, and the alcohol flowed free. They were coming toward the end of a fierce game of spades when Barbara slapped the winning card on the table.

A collective groan rose from the assemblage.

"I think she cheat," Ann Marie said. "Nobody can't win all the damned time."

Elizabth chuckled. "Don't hate, as the kids would say."

"All I got to say is that it's a damned good thing we don't play for money. I never win," Stephanie moaned.

Barbara got up from her seat. "I'm going to refill the ice tray so that you losers can continue to drown in your sorrows." She walked off laughing to herself and ignoring the names other than her own that were being hurled in her direction.

She went over to the refrigerator and opened the freezer just as Elizabeth came up behind her.

Elizabeth kept her voice low. "I didn't want to say anything yet, but Ron asked me to marry him."

"What!" Barbara squealed. "Oh my goodness, congratulations, sweetie."

"I'm so happy I could bust," she said, still whispering. "But for now it's just between me, you, and Ron."

"Sure."

Elizabeth ducked back out.

"Well, I'll be," Barbara murmured. She was pulling out the ice tray when Ann Marie popped her head in and came over to her.

"Don't say nutin' but guess who me daughter Raquel been tiptoeing with?"

Barbara couldn't begin to guess. "Who?"

"The damned security guard at the spa!"

"Drew Hawkins? Get out."

"But don't say nutin'. Raquel don't won nobody to know yet."

"Your secret is safe with me."

"Good. I knew it would be." She hurried back into the living room.

"At least he's a decent, good-looking man," she mumbled and banged the ice tray against the sink, just as Stephanie came in acting like she was looking for something.

She inched over to Barbara. "You gotta swear you won't say anything, not until I confirm it and go see my father and tell him."

"Your father! Steph—"

"Me and Tony are leaving to go see him in Texas next week." She beamed with delight.

Barbara wrapped her in a bear hug and held on. "Sis, I know how much this means to you."

"Yeah, it does." She stepped back, sniffed, and wiped her eyes. "Just promise not to say anything just yet."

"Cross my heart. But what is it that you have to confirm?"

"That I'm pregnant." She grinned, whirled away, and walked back inside.

Barbara grabbed a seat and sat down before she fell down. Although she kept a poker face she knew a little bit about Steph's father from Elizabeth. But a baby! She chuckled and shook her head. What was her crazy behind gonna do with a baby? Well, the kid would have three aunties to help out.

She pushed out a satisfied breath, got up, and finished putting the ice in the bucket. Well, the world had finally settled back on its axis and all things were good again. She picked up the bucket and tucked it under her arm. At least for the time being. She chuckled out loud. Yeah, at least for the time being.

* * * * *

Essence bestselling author Donna Hill
continues to wow Kimani Romance readers
with her sassy new miniseries!

Be sure to collect all of the titles in
Pause for Men:
Featuring four fabulously forty-something
divas who rewrite the book on romance

Here is a sneak peek at the blockbuster title
that started it all...

LOVE BECOMES HER
(Kimani Romance #5)

by Donna Hill

Chapter 1

The winds of change blew a nasty gust of havoc from one end of Morningside Drive to the other. It knocked over unchained garbage cans, rattled windows and stirred up unswept trash. As fate would have it, there were only a selected few whose doors were not only knocked on but kicked in.

Barbara Allen lifted the sheer white curtain from her third floor bedroom window and peeked outside. The sky was dull gray, the clouds as heavy as a maternity ward of expectant mothers. Stately brownstones were shrouded in fog, reminiscent of a scene out of an old English movie, but the lively radio voices of the KISS FM Wakeup Club playing in the background made the surreal come down to earth.

"Thank God it's Friday." She dropped the curtain back into place before sitting on the side of her bed.

She stuck her feet into her thick-soled white shoes, the third piece of her standard white ensemble. Finding something to wear five days a week hadn't been a problem for close to fifteen years. As a licensed rehabilitation therapist, white was de rigueur.

Barbara enjoyed her work at New York's Cornell University Medical Center. On the orthopedic unit where she worked, she'd met everyone from the grandmother with a hip replacement to the star athlete with a torn tendon.

She picked up her carryall bag from the foot of the bed and walked into her living room en route to the front door, but stopped short. Two empty wineglasses sat in proud accusation on her coffee table. A hot flash from the previous evening played with her mind: a little wine, some easy jazz, a cool breeze and a man young enough to be her son.

The alarm of her cell phone rang on her hip, its gentle vibration sending an unexpected thrill to shimmy down the inside of her thighs. It had been a long time if the vibration from a cell phone could get her going. Maybe she should have let that young boy stay the night. What he may have lacked in experience he could make up for with energy. She chuckled to herself at the ridiculousness of the notion and wondered what the girls would have to say. What she should have done was never let him within ten feet of her apartment in the first place. What had she been thinking? Hmmph, she knew what she'd been thinking. Fortunately, good sense prevailed and not a minute too soon.

Barbara gingerly picked up the glasses with the tips of her fingers as if they had the power to mysteriously conjure Michael up if she stroked them too hard—like a genie in a bottle. Holding them away from her body she went to the kitchen and deposited them in the sink, but not before being pulled into the watery remains that floated in the bottom of the glasses...warm hands, seductive words, sexual starvation…the kiss…almost. *Grrrr.* With a shake of her head she pushed the images aside, slung her bag onto her shoulder and headed out. She was much too old to be longing after that young boy as if he was dessert, she scolded herself while locking the front door. But if just thinking about him felt this good, then… *Barbara, don't let yourself get tripped up in those thoughts. Too long in the unholy state of abstinence must be frying your brain, girl.*

She trotted down the three flights of stairs, her standard shoulder-length ponytail bouncing behind her. She hurried passed the doors of her sleeping neighbors, careful when passing old man Carter's door so as not to stir up that maniac fox terrier of his that thought it was a pit bull. The dog was no bigger than a cat, but noisy enough to wake up the whole building. She chuckled to herself. If she didn't get caught in any unexpected traffic on FDR Drive she should arrive at the hospital in plenty of time to get some coffee and relax before her shift started at eight.

The hospital rehab ward was where she'd met

Michael Townsend six months earlier and where her current dilemma began.

He'd had surgery on his knee and was assigned to her for rehabilitation. Her job was to get him ready to resume his position with the NBA. His job, it seemed, was to get her in a position in his bed.

For the life of her, Barbara couldn't fathom why a young, gorgeous, wealthy man would be interested in her: a widow, old enough to be his mother and at least ten pounds overweight. Well…maybe five. Genetics played a big role in her smooth caramel-brown complexion, but was also responsible for her 42-inch hips and 40-C bustline. She was a solid size sixteen, and with her love of a good meal she knew, without careful monitoring, she could shoot past sixteen and keep right on going. Big women ran in her family on both sides like track stars trying to see who gets to the finish line first. Her mother and aunt on her father's side were in a constant dead heat.

Maybe that was it, she'd surmised. She was sure Michael must have some kind of mother-separation issue. But he'd told her on more than one occasion that he may have thought of her in a lot of ways, but mother never entered his mind.

She hadn't said a word to the girls about Michael and it was killing her. She wasn't sure if she'd resisted telling them out of embarrassment or afraid that they would all agree that she should give in and give it up! What would she do then? She knew she couldn't hold out much longer and she needed some advice other than her own.

The wind kicked up a notch as Barbara stepped outside. She hurried toward the corner where her car was parked, just as the first fat drop of rain hit her on the tip of the nose.

April, she thought.

By the time she got her ten-year-old Volvo warmed up enough to drive, rain danced furiously against everything it hit.

"This can't last," she muttered as she watched the wipers wage a fruitless battle against the deluge.

A sudden rapping on her window nearly had her drawing her last breath. She peered through the foggy driver's-side window then pressed the button to lower it.

"Stephanie! Damnit, you nearly scared me to death."

"Open up."

Barbara rolled her eyes and unlocked the doors.

Stephanie jumped in the backseat. "Whew. Almost drowned out there."

"What in the world are you doing going out this early? It's barely 7:00 a.m."

Stephanie laughed in that way of hers that made you believe that life was simply wonderful all the time. "Going out! Girl, I'm just coming in. Long night." She laughed again, followed by a delicate yawn.

Barbara shook her head in amazement. Stephanie Moore was the party girl of the quartet and at least four nights out of five she could be found in some nightclub or four-star restaurant with any one of an assortment of handsome, eligible and not-so-eligible men. *All work related*, she would insist during their weekly Friday-night soirees. And the remaining trio would regularly *umm-hmmm* her with raised brows of doubt.

Stephanie's job as senior publicist for H. L. Reuben & Associates, one of the most powerful

PR agencies in the country, was demanding on a variety of levels, the most demanding of which was keeping the company's high-profile, high-paying clients happy and scandal free. Suffice it to say, Stephanie was a pro who could put such a convincing spin on a bad situation that you would walk away believing that the bad situation was truly a blessing. And she had the looks to go with the job. She could have easily been a runway model and had done some print work right out of college, but felt it was not her true calling. But she maintained her flair for fashion and her makeup on clear, cinnamon-toned skin, framed with an expensive "I can't believe it's a weave," complete with strawberry-blond highlights that were always a showstopper. Stephanie Moore was a Tyra Banks look-alike without the big boobs.

"So who was it this time?" She glanced at Barbara in the rearview mirror and swore she saw a small bruise on the side of Stephanie's neck. It was then that she noticed that Stephanie was actually holding the top of her blouse together. "Steph…is everything okay?" She twisted around in her seat. Stephanie Moore may be a lot of things but disheveled, even at 7:00 a.m., was not one of them.

Stephanie brushed the water from her midthigh black skirt and crossed her long legs. "Yes. Fine. Tired, but fine." She brought her delicate hands toward her neck. "And to answer your other question, just another wannabe. Cute, though. Where are you headed?"

"Work. Where else?"

"Could you drop me off in front of my building? I need to get out of these wet clothes and take a nap. I was dozing in the cab, and the idiot cabdriver let me out too soon."

"Steph, you live three houses down."

"I know, but aren't you going that way?"

Barbara glanced at her friend again in the mirror. Dark circles rimmed the bottom of her lids as if her mascara had entered into the New York Marathon. "You coming over tonight?" she asked, cruising to stop in front of Stephanie's building.

"Wouldn't miss it. What are you fixing?"

"I thought I'd fix my pasta salad. Everyone seems to like it."

"Yum."

"What about you?"

"Wine, of course."

"Of course."

"I caught that note of sarcasm. Can I help it if you, Ann Marie and Ellie are better cooks than I am? No sense in disappointing you guys with my hopeless dishes." She puckered her lips. "That was one of Brian's biggest complaints. I was great in bed, wonderful to look at but I couldn't boil an egg. Go figure." She shrugged in her patent dismissive fashion, but her tone lacked its usual sass. "His loss." She popped the car door open. "Thanks, Barb. See you tonight."

Before Barbara could respond or ask the questions that hovered on the tip of her tongue, Stephanie had darted out of sight and into her building. For a moment she sat there wondering just what kind of night Stephanie had really had. She turned on the radio and slowly drove off.

She often wished she was more like Stephanie: carefree, secure in her sexuality and not caring much what others thought of her and her choices. Unfortunately she was the polar opposite, hence her dilemma about Michael. And maybe it was just as well.

Barbara arrived with only fifteen minutes to spare before she had to clock in. She went directly to the staff lounge hoping against hope that a fresh pot of coffee would be there to welcome her.

No such luck.

Mildly annoyed, she fished around in the cabinet and took out a can of coffee, determined to get one cup down before what she knew would be a long day ahead.

Just as she poured four scoops of coffee into the coffeemaker, her cell phone rang and not the alarm this time. She glanced down at the tiny, sleek gadget on her hip and saw Elizabeth's number on the illuminated face. She smiled, snatched it up and pressed the green telephone icon.

"Ellie, hi, what's up?"

"I'm gonna kill him!" came the ear-piercing voice, followed by the most heart-wrenching sobs Barbara had ever heard.

Barbara jerked back from the phone in alarm. She frowned, lowered her head and her voice. "Ellie, calm down and tell me what's wrong." Elizabeth Lewis was one of the most stable, sensible women that Barbara knew. She was never ruffled or derailed by unforeseen events. Ellie was the one who held Barbara's hand and her head when her husband, Marvin, died. It was Ellie who was the calm during and after the storm, the only one of the quartet who Barbara felt comfortable telling her deepest secrets to…well, except the Michael thing. So, to hear Ellie come unglued truly meant that the stars were misaligned.

"I know you don't mean that, and who are you talking about? It can't be Matt. I—"

"Don't you dare mention that bastard's name!"

So it was Matt. "Okay," she said gingerly. "Why don't you tell me what happened. I'm sure—"

"After twenty-five years, twenty-five fucking years of my life I give to him and he does this to me!"

Her voice had reached operatic octaves and Barbara still had no clue as to what the "nameless bastard" had done. A door slammed in the background, followed by the sound of shattering glass. *This was serious.*

"Ellie, I can't help you if you don't tell me what's going on."

Elizabeth sniffed hard. "I...I have to get ready for my appointment. I'm sorry for calling you like a crazy person," she said, smoothly sliding back into her calm, in-control self. "I'll see you tonight."

The call disconnected, leaving Barbara standing there more confused than when she first heard Ellie's tirade. She slid the phone back into the case on her hip.

"Barb..."

She turned toward the door. It was her assistant, Sheila.

"Your first patient is here."

"Thanks. I'll be right there." She looked at the percolating coffee, down at her cell phone and then the door. "And it's only eight o'clock," she muttered, walking out.

Fortunately, the rest of her day had been pure routine, Barbara mused as she did a final check of her two-bedroom apartment. The food was on the warming tray in the living room, the salad was freshly tossed and sitting in the fridge. Stephanie was bringing the wine, Ellie was always good for dessert and Ann Marie was the Caribbean-cuisine queen. She was sure to add some island flavor to their evening. Their favorite jazz station played softly in the background and a brand-new deck of playing cards sat ceremoniously in the center of the table.

She placed her hands on her hips—satisfied. They should be arriving shortly, she thought. Ann Marie was usually the first to arrive. She had a real thing about being early and was always willing to lend a hand with any last-minute doings.

As if she'd conjured her up, Ann Marie rang the doorbell.

"It's raining cats and dogs and *daughters*," she said, shaking out her umbrella and dumping it in the wastebasket that Barbara used for such occasions.

She helped Ann Marie out of her trench coat. "And daughters?"

Ann Marie turned toward Barbara, and her younger-than-her-years face pinched into a pained expression.

"Raquel turned up on me doorstep last night, complete with suitcases and a long story about leaving 'er 'usband."

"What?"

"You 'eard me," she said, sounding more annoyed than concerned about her daughter's current state of marital un-bliss, her Jamaican accent in full force. She marched off into the living room. "I need a drink."

"Help yourself." She followed Ann Marie inside, noting the three-inch heels. Ann Marie was the only woman she knew who wore high heels to the supermarket. Perhaps it had something to do with the fact that in bare feet, Ann Marie was no more than five feet tall.

Ann Marie pulled a bottle of Courvoisier right out of her Gucci bag, took the top off like a pro and poured herself a healthy glass before Barbara could blink. She marched off to the couch and plopped down, then looked up at Barbara.

"Can you believe it? She's moving back in with me for heaven's sake. What me gon' do?"

"What are you going to do? What about Raquel?"

She sucked her teeth and waved her hand. "Raquel will be fine at some point. The question is, will I?" She took a long swallow of her drink that made Barbara wince, then began rambling in that rapid-fire way of hers, with her accent so thick you needed a translator to interpret.

Barbara held up her hands. "Hold it, hold it. I'm really not understanding a word you're saying, Ann Marie."

Ann Marie paused, dragged in a deep breath and looked up at Barbara with wide, imploring brown eyes set in a rich chocolate–brown face. She ran her hand through her bone-straight mid-shoulder-length hair. "How in the world am I supposed to get my groove on with my twenty-three-year-old daughter listening to dear old mom knocking boots in the next room? I'm not the church mouse on the block, if you know what I mean."

Barbara let out a bark of nervous laughter. If that was the worst of Ann Marie's problems, she ain't heard nothing yet. Tonight was going to be more than a little interesting.

Chapter 2

Barbara wasn't quite sure what to say to Ann Marie at the moment, while she gulped down her drink and quickly refilled her glass without taking a breath. So Barbara opted not to press the issue. Knowing Ann Marie, she'd spill it all before the night was over.

"I'm going to start putting the stuff out. Ellie and Steph should be here any minute."

"I'll help you." She put the top back on the bottle, shoved it back down inside her purse then

pushed herself up from the chair. "Oh lawd."
She slapped her palm to her forehead.

"What?"

"Left de damn curry chicken right in de car.
Chile got me so upset, can't t'ink straight."

Barbara chuckled as Ann Marie snatched up
her umbrella and darted back outside. She took
the salad out of the fridge and put it on the
counter next to the dressings. She always did a
buffet-style dinner, so everyone was on their own
to get what they wanted when they wanted it. She
took a quick look around. Ice filled the ice
bucket, there was a case of Coors Light in the
cooler for Stephanie and four bottles of wine to
supplement the wine that Stephanie had
promised to bring, for everyone else. But appar-
ently Ann Marie had other plans. Hmm. She'd
never known Ann Marie to be a hard drinker and
certainly not one to actually carry a bottle of
liquor stashed in her purse. The sudden arrival of
Raquel must have truly rocked unshakable Ann.

Raquel had been out on her own right out of
high school, which Barbara personally thought
was much too young, but Ann Marie was

adamant about Raquel standing on her own two feet and being a woman. "Can't be having no two grown-ass women in one house," Ann Marie had said. "Make for bad business. I'm the only queen in me castle. Ain't sharing no throne."

From the day Raquel moved into a small studio somewhere in Brooklyn, Barbara had seen her maybe five times in all those years. One of which had been at her wedding. She'd been a beautiful bride. It appeared as if her husband, Earl, loved the ground Raquel walked on. What was so odd about that day was that Ann Marie seemed more relieved than anything else, as if now that Raquel was a married woman, whatever semblance of care and responsibility she had for her daughter was no longer anything she had to concern herself with. Ann Marie barely spoke of her, as if she were no more than some distant relative as opposed to her only child.

Sad, Barbara thought. It was the one thing she'd always wanted in her life, a child of her own. Someone to love and nourish and watch grow up and become a wonderful human being. In her case, that was never to be. She knew that if she'd ever had children she would have spoiled them rotten and bragged about them to everyone who would listen. Ann Marie, on the other hand…

The doorbell chimed.

Ann Marie held a large tray in her hands and the mouthwatering aroma seeping out from beneath the foil made Barbara's stomach knot in anticipation. If there was one thing Ann Marie could do and do well, it was cook. The girl put her foot in it every time. And right behind her was Elizabeth.

Elizabeth hurried in with her tray, as well. "Red velvet cake tonight, ladies."

"Oh my. What's the occasion?" Barbara stepped aside to let her friends in. "You only do red velvet for something major." She shut the door and the bell rang again. She snatched it back open.

"Damn, just close the door in my face. I know I only bring wine but I still can beat all y'all in spades."

Barbara laughed. "Sorry, girl, I didn't see you."

"Yeah, yeah." She stepped in and took off her Burberry trench coat and hung it up on the rack in the hall.

She looks much better than this morning, Barbara quickly observed, shutting the door for the final time. Maybe it was just the rain that had her looking so out of sorts. She went into the living room where Ann Marie and Ellie were already seated around the coffee table, snacking on celery sticks and dip.

"Y'all don't waste any time," Steph said, announcing her arrival, then taking a seat next to Ellie on the couch. She reached for a carrot. "How's everyone doing?" She took a delicate bite and looked from one woman to the next.

Ellie sighed.

Ann Marie sucked her teeth and rolled her eyes.

"Damn, what did I do?" Stephanie asked.

"Nothing," they muttered in unison.

Steph glanced up at Barbara for some kind of hint as to what was going on, but Barbara only shrugged in response. "I'll get the wine."

"Bring plenty," Ellie said.

Ann Marie got up and followed Barbara into the kitchen. She lowered her voice. "Don't say nutin' to dem about Raquel just yet. Okay?"

Barbara looked at her, perplexed. "Fine, but why not?"

"Me really don't wan' talk 'bout it tonight. Still too pissed and upset."

"Ann, it really—"

Ellie walked in. "What's taking so long? And what are you two whispering about?"

"Nutin'." Ann Marie took two bottles of wine and the ice bucket then walked out.

Ellie watched her leave. "What's with her?"

"I wish I knew." She put her hands on her hips. "The question is, what's with you? What was that phone call about this morning? You had me worried."

"I can't talk about it right now." Her eyes suddenly filled and she sniffed loudly. "It's just so fucking awful." Her mouth trembled and she covered it with her hand.

That was the second time in one day that Ellie had cursed. It was something she didn't do and it sounded like a foreign language coming out of her mouth.

"Ell." She put her hand on Elizabeth's shoulder. "What is it, sweetie?"

She just shook her head. Just then, Stephanie burst into the room.

"Ann Marie forgot the Coors. Are they in the

freezer? You know I like mine icy cold," Steph chattered, oblivious to the cloud of tension in the room.

Ellie sucked in a breath and darted for the bathroom down the hall.

Steph frowned then put her hands on her hips. "What is wrong with everybody tonight? Feel like I'm at a wake and no one told me."

"Probably the crappy weather."

"I guess." Steph sounded unconvinced. She stepped closer to Barbara. "Listen, about this morning. I'd really appreciate it if you didn't say anything to the girls."

"Wouldn't think of it," Barbara said. *What's one more secret among friends?*

Second chance for romance...

When
Valentines
Collide

Award-winning author
ADRIANNE
BYRD

Therapists Chante and Michael Valentine agree to a "sex-therapy" retreat to save their marriage. At first the seminar revives their passion—but their second chance at love is threatened when a devastating secret is revealed.

"Byrd proves again that she's a wonderful storyteller."
—*Romantic Times BOOKreviews* on *The Beautiful Ones*

Available the first week of February,
wherever books are sold.

KIMANI
ROMANCE

www.kimanipress.com

KPAB0050207

A dramatic story of danger and adventure
set in the depths of Africa...

IN THE
LIGHT of
LOVE

Bestselling Arabesque author

Deborah
Fletcher Mello

Working together in a war-torn African nation where danger
lurked everywhere, Talisa London and Dr. Jericho Becton
were swept up in a wave of desire that left them breathless.
But would they survive their mission with their love—
and lives—intact?

Available the first week of February, wherever books are sold.

KIMANI
ROMANCE

Where had all the magic gone?

FOREVER, FOR ALWAYS, FOR LOVE

Award-winning author
KIM SHAW

Determined to rekindle the passion in her
failing marriage, Josette Crawford undergoes a major
makeover. But when life changes threaten to derail her
love train, she and hubby, Seth, wonder whether their
love is strong enough to keep them together forever.

*Available the first week of February,
wherever books are sold.*

KIMANI™
ROMANCE

www.kimanipress.com   KPKS0070207

A brand-new story of love
and drama from...

national bestselling author

MARCIA
KING-GAMBLE

All
ABOUT
ME

Big-boned beauty Chere Adams
plunges into an extreme makeover
to capture the eye of fitness fanatic
Quentin Abraham—but the more
she changes, the less he seems to
notice her. Is it possible Quentin's
more interested in the old Chere?

*Available the first week of January
wherever books are sold.*

KIMANI™
ROMANCE

Winning her love wouldn't be so easy
the second time around...

HERE
and
NOW

Favorite author
Michelle Monkou

When Chase Dillard left Laura Masterson years ago to pursue
his Olympic dreams, he broke her heart. Now that they're
working together, Chase has lots of ground to make up if he
wants to win her back.

KIMANI™
ROMANCE

www.kimanipress.com   KPMM0020107